Creatures

Who's Been Sitting in My Chair?

"Opal!" Not knowing whether to feel relieved or annoyed, Rhoda started towards the armchair.

Then suddenly, in the cushioned depths of the chair's seat, a pair of eyes appeared.

There was nothing else. No face, no shape; just *eyes*. They were almond-shaped, amber-yellow, and had huge black pupils that glared furiously at Rhoda.

The purring stopped. There was an instant's absolute silence – then a piercing animal screech ripped through the room, an appalling din that battered Rhoda's ears. Her mouth opened in the beginnings of a terrified scream—

**Look for other Creatures titles
by Louise Cooper:**

Creatures

Who's Been Sitting in My Chair?

Louise Cooper

Scholastic Children's Books
Commonwealth House, 1–19 New Oxford Street,
London WC1A 1NU, UK
London ~ New York ~ Toronto ~ Sydney ~ Auckland
Mexico City ~ New Delhi ~ Hong Kong
First published by Scholastic Ltd, 1999

ISBN 0 590 11390 9

Typeset by Falcon Oast Graphic Art
Printed by Cox & Wyman Ltd, Reading, Berks

2 4 6 8 10 9 7 5 3 1

1

When Dad stopped the car outside the gate of the new house, Mum turned round to see Rhoda's rear end sticking up in the air as she scrabbled frantically with something in the luggage compartment behind the back seat.

"Rhoda, what are you *doing*?" Mum asked, astonished.

Rhoda started to mumble a reply, but was interrupted by a raucous noise from somewhere among the bags and cases. There was a scuffle, a hiss followed by a squawk; then Rhoda turned herself the right way up. Her face was scarlet and her short, dark hair looked like a haystack. In her arms was a very indignant Siamese cat.

"She got out of the carrying-cage again," said Rhoda apologetically. She peered back over the seat. "And she's been sick."

"Oh, *wonderful!*" Mum pulled a face. "Well, you'll have to clear it up – the removal van'll be here any minute, and Dad and I are going to be much too busy." She opened the car door. "I've got the house keys. Take Opal inside. And this time, make sure that cage is shut properly!"

Hauling cases from the back of the car, her parents set off up the garden path. Rhoda pushed the protesting Opal back into her travelling cage, then paused and took a long, careful look at her new home. It was the end one of a row of three houses, standing alone in the quiet village lane, and there was something cottagey and almost chocolate-boxy about it. Small windows, a sway-backed roof, and a dinky little front garden. The garden was very overgrown; even though it was only the beginning of April there were plants sprawling everywhere, like mad green fur. Rhoda liked it instantly. It had a personality, she thought; and

2

the way the door and windows were arranged was like a face. Apparently it had been empty for nearly a year, and to Rhoda's imaginative mind the "face" had a sad, lonely look, as if it had given up hope that anyone would ever love it again.

"Hello, house," Rhoda said, smiling. "Cheer up – we're your new humans, and we'll soon bring you back to life!"

Mum and Dad had disappeared inside, and she followed them up the path. The joggling of the cage annoyed Opal, and she started to swear loudly as only Siamese cats can. A net curtain twitched in the next house. Rhoda glimpsed a face peering out of the window, then the curtain dropped again and moments later the house's front door opened.

A blond-haired boy of about Rhoda's age stood on the doorstep. He grinned at her and said, "Hi. Whatever have you got in there?"

"My cat." Rhoda grinned back, a bit sheepishly. "She doesn't like travelling."

"A cat. Ah." The boy's tone changed; he sounded suddenly uneasy, and to Rhoda's puzzlement he added, "What *kind* of cat?"

"She's a Siamese." The question, or perhaps

3

more the way he said it, seemed weird to Rhoda, but before she could ask if he had some kind of a problem, his face cleared and he said, "Oh, Siamese, right!" A grin almost of relief spread across his face. "You're the new neighbours, then?"

"Looks like it."

"Well, you can't be any worse than the last one!" He came out into the garden, shoving his hands into his jeans pockets and leaning on the low, rickety fence. "I'm Danny Downing, and I've got two older brothers, a tortoise and a lousy school report."

Rhoda laughed. "Rhoda Mackay. No brothers, no sisters, one cat and I'm not much good at school either!"

Opal made a rude remark from the depths of the cage, and Danny asked, "So what brings you to this dump?"

Rhoda looked around her, and felt a sudden desire to defend the new house. "It's not a dump!" she said. "I like it."

"Wait till you've been living here for a while," Danny told her. "Nothing to do, nowhere to go, no buses – you name it, we haven't got it! And the electricity goes off every

4

time there's a thunderstorm, so we have to use candles."

"I like candlelight," Rhoda said, still defensively. "It makes things look so different – sort of magical, as if you'd stepped back into the past." She was about to add that she often wished she *could* go back into the past, and see the world as it used to be before things like electric lights were invented. But the expression on Danny's face stopped her. He looked bemused, almost horrified, and Rhoda turned her face away to hide a smile. Danny was the down-to-earth type, all right. Oh, well; it couldn't be helped. And he seemed OK enough in other ways.

A voice from inside the house shouted, "Rho, what are you doing out there? Come and give us a hand!"

"I'd better go," said Rhoda. Opal agreed loudly, and Danny grinned again. "See you later, maybe. Good luck with the dump – and the cat!"

He went into his own house and shut the door. Rhoda stood still for a few seconds, thinking about candles and history and wondering vaguely what Danny had meant about them not being any worse than the last neighbour. Then she shrugged, and hurried up the path.

The removal van was late, and by the time it arrived Rhoda had had plenty of opportunity to explore her new home.

The house was as chocolate-boxy inside as out. All the doors had latches instead of handles, there were beams and a big open fire-place in the sitting-room, and the stairs were so steep and twisty and narrow that Mum was convinced they'd have to take out the upstairs windows to get the beds in. Exploring the main bedroom, Rhoda found to her delight that someone, sometime in the past, had pinned up a lot of pictures of cats, mostly cut out from magazines, though with some proper photographs among them. They looked quite old, and though they were faded and curling at the edges she resolved to rescue the best ones and add them to her own cat album.

"Oh, yes," said Mum when she saw the pictures. "They must have been Mrs Wilson's — that's the old lady who used to live here."

Rhoda studied a black-and-white photo

which showed a fat cat with tabby-looking markings sitting in what she presumed was the house's own garden. A tall, thin woman in old-fashioned clothes was blurrily visible in the background.

"Is she dead now?" she asked.

"Who, Mrs Wilson? No, but she's very old; over eighty, I think. She couldn't look after herself any more, so she went into a home. That's why the house was sold; to pay for her care."

"That's sad," said Rhoda.

"Yes, it is," Mum agreed. "But she's a widow, without any family, so I suppose she didn't have much choice."

"Did she have a cat?"

"I've no idea," said Mum. "We didn't meet her; we just dealt with the estate agent." She glanced at Rhoda, knowing what she was thinking, and smiled. "Don't worry. If she did, I'm sure someone will have looked after it."

The cat pictures weren't the only things of Mrs Wilson's that had been left behind. The house clearers had been in and had taken most of the furniture away – but in the kitchen they found two old tables and an armchair.

"I suppose they weren't worth bothering with," Dad said as he examined them. "The tables are useless, anyway – they're riddled with woodworm. But the chair's not too bad. In fact if it was re-upholstered, it'd look quite good in the sitting-room. Might even be a bit of an antique."

Mum pressed the cushioned seat. "It feels comfortable," she said. "And it's got that cottagey look that goes with the house. Let's keep it."

They carried the chair through to the sitting-room and put it beside the fireplace. It looked right there, Rhoda thought. As if it belonged. Probably it had been Mrs Wilson's favourite chair, and she imagined the old lady sitting in it, with her cat (Rhoda had decided now that Mrs Wilson *must* have had a cat) purring on her lap.

As if summoned up by that thought, Opal came slinking round the stairs door. She had been let out of her cage, though not out of the house, and was exploring everything thoroughly. Tail in the air, she strolled towards the chair – then stopped.

"There you are, Opal." Rhoda said. She

plonked herself in the armchair and patted her knees. "Come and try it out."

Opal's whiskers twitched and she stared. Normally she didn't need asking twice when anyone invited her to sit on them, but this time she didn't move.

"Come on, Opal," Rhoda cajoled. "Lap!"

Opal's vivid blue eyes flashed with what seemed to be anger, and she gave a low growl. Then, to everyone's surprise, her lips drew back and she hissed loudly before turning tail and running into the kitchen.

"Well!" said Mum. "What's got into her?"

"Fussy little madam," Dad commented. "What does she expect – a gilded throne with a velvet cushion on it?"

"It probably smells strange to her," Mum pointed out. "Never mind. If it's one piece of furniture we can keep free of cat hairs, I'll be well pleased!"

Opal had disappeared, but Rhoda could hear her grumbling behind the kitchen door, and a strange, cold little realization crept into her mind. Mum and Dad probably hadn't noticed it, but when Opal had growled and hissed, she hadn't been looking at the chair or even at

Rhoda. Instead, she had been staring at a spot *beyond* the chair, at floor level. As if she had seen something that wasn't visible to human eyes. Something that shouldn't have been there.

Something that had *scared* her. . .

Uneasily, Rhoda let her gaze slide sideways to the floor. But there was nothing strange about it. It was just an ordinary floor, with the old, bare boards scuffed and scratched where furniture had once stood.

And yet. . .

The sudden roar of an engine outside made her jump, and the thought that had been forming in her mind skittered away as she looked up to see the removal van pulling to a halt at the gate.

"About time, too!" Mum was at the window. "Rho, you'd better put Opal back in her cage while the furniture's brought in. Then the *very* first thing I'm going to do is dig out the kettle and make some coffee at long last!"

2

The next few hours were hectic, but at last the furniture was all in, the van had gone, and they were ready to start putting the house in order.

Opal was thoroughly fed up by this time. She had been stuck in her cage while all the turmoil and activity went on around her, and when she was let out at last she was promptly – and probably deliberately – sick again, this time on the kitchen floor. Rhoda cleared up the mess, then decided that what Opal needed was something to cheer her up. So she buckled on the cat's little leather harness, clipped her long lead to it, and took her out into the back garden.

The back garden was long and narrow, and as overgrown as the front. Another rickety fence separated it from the Downings' next door, and a path ran down the middle to a derelict potting-shed. There was an apple tree (Opal would love climbing that) and when Rhoda looked closely she found two frayed and broken pieces of very ancient rope tied around one of the branches, as if a swing or hammock had once hung there.

Opal picked her way through the tangle on delicate, chocolate-brown paws, making interested remarks and stopping every few seconds to sniff around. Suddenly she tensed, flattening her ears. Her tail lashed excitedly, she dropped to a crouch – then made a flying pounce into a bush. The lead jerked, yanking Rhoda along with it, and as she stumbled after Opal, Rhoda almost fell over a dark hummock in the bush's shadows.

The hummock was a large tortoise. It had drawn back into its shell as Opal leaped, and now the cat was dabbing and batting at it, trying to work out where its head and legs had gone.

"Opal, get off!" Rhoda scolded. "Leave it alone!"

Opal *wowled* in frustration as she was hauled away, and a voice from the other side of the fence said, "Have you found Moses? Oh, brilliant!"

It was Danny. He scrambled over the fence and dived to retrieve the tortoise. Straightening up, he grinned at Rhoda. "Moses only came out of hibernation last week, and he keeps getting out of our garden and coming in here," he explained. "It's too cold to leave him out overnight, and guess who gets the job of finding him!"

Moses poked his head out of his shell, didn't think much of what he saw, and ducked back in again. Rhoda said, "I was just showing Opal the garden. Opal, say hi to Danny."

Opal went towards Danny – and quickly, reflexively, Danny backed away a step. He hadn't meant to, Rhoda saw; it was an instinct, and it happened before he could stop himself. Then he froze, standing still and staring down as Opal sniffed at his trainers. The cat looked up at him and made an inquiring noise. Danny laughed – sort of – and then suddenly he relaxed again and bent to stroke her. Opal arched her back with pleasure and started to purr, and in a voice that sounded just a bit *too* casual Danny said:

"She's friendlier than that great fat tabby Mrs Wilson used to have. If I had a quid for every time that thing hissed or spat at me, I'd be rich by now."

Rhoda's eyes lit with interest and she forgot his weird reaction. "Mrs Wilson did have a cat, then? There are hundreds of cat pictures in the house – I thought she must have liked them."

"*Liked* them?" Danny echoed, and laughed. "She was completely potty about them! That tabby – Sheba, she called it – she treated it like her own kid. Fussing it, cuddling it, talking to it all the time as if it could understand. She probably fed it on cream and smoked salmon, too. Totally nuts."

"There's nothing wrong with talking to cats," Rhoda said, a little huffily. "I talk to Opal. And *I* think she understands a lot of what I say."

Danny shrugged. "Maybe. But you're not barmy enough to think she talks back to you, are you? To hear old Mrs W go on, you'd think her precious Sheba had a degree in English!

14

'Sheba says this', and 'Sheba says that' – oh yeah, and her favourite one: 'Sheba says you're a horrible boy and she doesn't like you.'"

Rhoda's mouth twitched. "Ah. So you didn't get on with her, then."

Danny's eyebrows went up. "You'd have had to be a saint to get on with the old bat! She was always complaining about something. And she *really* had it in for me. I'm not kidding, the day she went into that home, I felt like having a party!"

"Oh, well. . ." Rhoda struggled to be fair. "She was old. . . Maybe she couldn't help being crotchety." She paused. "What happened to her cat when she went?"

"It had died a few months before," Danny told her. "It was ancient, anyway. We all thought she'd get another one – everyone said she'd never been without a cat before. But she didn't. I suppose she knew she wouldn't be here for much longer, so she didn't bother."

For the second time that day Rhoda felt a pang of sadness for Mrs Wilson. However awkward and grumpy she was, the fact that she had loved her cat so much proved that she had

15

feelings. Sheba's death must have broken her heart. And the knowledge that she would soon also have to leave her house would have made her feel even worse.

"The home she went into," she said musingly. "Is it somewhere near here?"

"I think so," Danny replied. "Mum knows the name of it – she sent on the post for a while. Why?"

"Oh . . . nothing, really. It was just a thought I had, but it isn't important." Rhoda didn't want to tell Danny any more, for she knew he would only laugh at her. But she wanted to get the home's address, and do a kindness for Mrs Wilson. Just a small thing, but she had the feeling that the old lady would be pleased.

Danny said suddenly, "I'd better take Moses indoors before it gets too cold. What are you doing tomorrow?"

"Helping Mum and Dad get the house straight, I suppose." Rhoda looked up at him, pushing her idea aside for the time being. "Then maybe a bit of exploring, round the village."

"There's not much to explore. But if you want a guide. . .?"

She hesitated a moment, then smiled. "Yes. Why not?"

"OK." Danny grinned broadly. "See you tomorrow, then. I'll call for you in the morning. 'Bye."

"'Bye." Rhoda watched as, carrying Moses, he climbed back over the fence and went into his house. When he had gone, everything seemed very quiet and still. Dusk was gathering, and when she listened hard there wasn't a sound to be heard anywhere. As if the whole world had already gone to sleep.

A soft spring breeze blew up, ruffling her hair and making the overgrown bushes in the garden rustle faintly. A bough on the apple tree creaked. Rhoda thought about cats, and sadness, and other people's lives. Then she picked up Opal, who had settled at her feet, and went slowly indoors.

The door closed behind her. For a minute or so nothing disturbed the stillness. Then swiftly, silently, a shadow glided across the garden, and paused for a moment where Rhoda had stood, before slipping away into the deepening darkness.

By the time she went to bed that night, Rhoda was nearly asleep on her feet. But despite her tiredness, she felt a sense of satisfaction. They had all spent the evening unpacking and arranging things, and by the time they finished the house really was beginning to look and feel like home. Rhoda's bedroom overlooked the back garden, and the window had a deep sill which she could sit on. Opal had already discovered the sill, and decided – as Opal often did – that it was Hers. When Rhoda climbed into bed the cat was stretched smugly along the length of it, leaving no room for anyone or anything else, and when Rhoda turned the light off the sound of her purring seemed to fill the room.

The first night in a new house was always strange and Rhoda half expected to lie awake for hours. She didn't; in fact she fell asleep very quickly. But it wasn't a deep sleep, and several times during the night she woke up again. On the first two occasions she heard Opal still purring on the sill; then on the third she felt a small, warm weight on her hip. Not bothering to open her eyes, Rhoda smiled and murmured, "Hello, Opal."

The purring sound was her only answer. It still seemed to be coming from the direction of the window – which it couldn't be, of course, as Opal was very definitely on the bed. Funny, Rhoda thought vaguely, the Siamese hardly ever did that; in fact she couldn't remember the last time it had happened. Opal disdained beds; she preferred to have a sleeping place all to herself. Oh, well. Animals were affected by new surroundings, too, so probably Opal just wanted some reassurance.

Rhoda settled back to sleep. The purring continued, and as she drifted off it seemed to grow louder, a steady, thrumming drone. *Louder . . . louder . . . droning. . .*

Rhoda began to dream. . .

She was going downstairs, but she wasn't walking. Instead she seemed to float, as if she was as light as a feather. Her feet weren't touching the stairs, and the door at the bottom looked a very long way away, but she wasn't afraid. It seemed like the most natural thing in the world.

In the room below, Opal was purring. She was making so much noise that she was sure to wake Mum and Dad, so Rhoda was going down to tell her to be quiet. Drifting to the foot of the stairs, she reached out and lifted the door latch. The door opened, and as the moonlit room was revealed Rhoda frowned.

Where was all the furniture? The room was completely empty – but they'd spent hours getting everything arranged, she knew they had!

She stood in the middle of the floor, staring around bewilderedly. Whatever had happened to all their things? And where was Opal? The purring sound was deafening now, but there was no sign of the Siamese cat.

"Opal?" she called out. "Opal, where are you?"

No answer. Rhoda turned round in a full circle, looking. And when she faced the hearth again, she saw something that hadn't been there before.

It was the old chair that they'd found when they moved in. The moonlight fell directly on it, lighting it like a spotlamp, and in the irrational way of dreams Rhoda noticed that it wasn't quite in the place where Dad had put it, but closer to the fireplace.

And the noise of Opal's purring seemed to be coming from the chair seat.

"Opal!" Not knowing whether to feel relieved or annoyed, Rhoda started towards the armchair.

Then suddenly, in the cushioned depths of the chair's seat, a pair of eyes appeared.

There was nothing else. No face, no shape; just *eyes*. They were almond-shaped, amber-yellow, and had huge black pupils that glared furiously at Rhoda.

The purring stopped. There was an instant's absolute silence – then a piercing animal screech ripped through the room, an appalling din that battered Rhoda's ears. Her mouth opened in the beginnings of a terrified scream—

And she jolted awake, to find herself out of bed and on her feet, with hands splayed and nose pressed to the wall of her new bedroom.

3

Rhoda was badly shaken by the dream. But she was even more worried by the sleepwalking.

As far as she knew she had never, ever sleepwalked in her life – so why had it happened now? This was *frightening*. Was there something horribly wrong with her? Was she going crazy? Or was it just a side-effect of the dream and her strange new surroundings?

She didn't sleep again for the rest of the night, and got up soon after dawn. Opal, who was back on the window ledge, raised her head at the sound of the bedroom door opening, and with an eager chirrup followed Rhoda out on to the landing. Rhoda shivered as she saw the stairwell and remembered her nightmare. Floating, like a ghost . . . it had been a weird feeling, and even now it gave her a dizzy lurch just to think about it.

With Opal at her heels she went downstairs and opened the door to the sitting-room. The curtains hadn't been put up yet and the dim morning light made everything look pearly-coloured and unreal. Uneasily Rhoda glanced at the armchair, but nothing had happened to it; it hadn't mysteriously changed or anything.

Except. . .

She paused, frowning. There *was* something different about the chair, she was sure. But what? The red velvet cushion Mum had put on it last night was still there, so it couldn't be that. But something. . .

Then it clicked. The chair wasn't where Dad had placed it. It had moved closer to the fire-place.

Just like in her dream.

A surge of fright welled up in Rhoda – then collapsed as she realized how idiotic she was being. The chair hadn't moved, of course; it had *been* moved. Mum or Dad must have decided that it wasn't quite right where it was, and they'd shifted it after she went to bed. She was getting the jitters over absolutely nothing. In fact when she looked closer she could see that the chair's legs were now positioned fairly and squarely over the old scuffed marks on the floorboards. This must be where it used to stand when Mrs Wilson lived here, and Mum and Dad had seen the marks and decided to put it back in its old place. As simple as that.

It was odd, though, that she should have dreamed of seeing the chair in the place it used to occupy. Like a kind of telepathy, as if her mind had unconsciously known what Mum and Dad were doing. Or as if she had somehow looked back into the past, as she so often imagined being able to do. Rhoda smiled to herself, feeling better. She'd had a weird dream, that was all. It probably wouldn't happen again, and neither would the sleep-walking. Even if they did, it didn't necessarily mean there was anything wrong. Just a phase, as Mum would have said. Mum put most things Rhoda did down to "phases".

She turned to go into the kitchen to make

herself some coffee . . . and saw Opal. The cat was at the foot of the stairs. She hadn't come into the room; instead she was crouching on the bottom step, her tail swinging from side to side and her blue eyes narrowed to ferocious little slits.

"Opal?" said Rhoda. Usually Opal was in the kitchen and loudly demanding breakfast the moment anyone got up. "What's up, Opie? What's the matter?"

Opal looked up at her and gave a raucous Siamese yowl. She sounded extremely cross – and suddenly Rhoda guessed why.

"You haven't worked out where the kitchen is yet, have you?" She started to laugh, then smothered it in case Opal's dignity was offended. "It's not in its usual place, and you're annoyed!" Bending down, she tickled Opal between her ears. "Come on. Kitchen's this way. I'll open a tin of your favourite food."

She walked into the kitchen, knowing the cat would follow her. Opal did – but as she jumped down from the step, she also did something else. Rhoda's back was turned, so she didn't see what happened. But Opal paused as she crossed the floor. She looked back at the armchair. And she bared her teeth in a silent snarl that was half fear and half challenge.

Then with a sudden rush she darted into the kitchen after Rhoda, as if some invisible presence was chasing her.

It started to rain during breakfast, and by the time Danny came round it was teeming down, putting paid to any idea of exploring the village. Danny didn't seem to mind and offered to help with the unpacking, which as Dad said was probably going to take a month of Sundays. The offer was gladly accepted, and as the two of them got down to work Rhoda discovered why he had been so eager.

"I'm just being nosy," Danny admitted cheerfully, as he dragged a cardboard box full of ornaments across the sitting-room floor. "I've never been inside this house before, so I wanted to see what it was like."

"Oh, right. So it's not out of the kindness of your heart then?" Rhoda grinned.

"No way!" He paused and looked around. "It's totally different to our place. They look the same on the outside, but ours is much more modernized; we covered up all the beams and stuff. This is like something out of the Ark!"

Rhoda shrugged. "Mum and Dad like it. So do I. Everyone's different."

"I suppose. So, have you found any hidden treasure yet? Or secret doors with skeletons walled up behind them?"

He was sending her up, and Rhoda flicked him a scowl. "Come on; it's not *that* old!"

"Old enough. The little kids at the end house used to think Mrs Wilson was a witch. You know, with a cauldron instead of a cooker in the kitchen. They reckoned she had a secret place under the floorboards, where she kept her pointy hat and her broomstick and her book of spells. Once, they kicked their football over the fence and bashed down one of her favourite plants. They went round for days after that terrified she'd turn them into frogs!"

Rhoda wouldn't have minded betting that she knew who'd put the idea of witches in the little kids' heads, but she only said, "Well, we haven't found anything like that. And if there are any pointy hats or broomsticks under the floorboards, they can stay there – we're having fitted carpets."

They finished lugging the box into place and

Danny unwrapped ornaments while Rhoda arranged them on the shelves of Mum's display cabinet. A minute or two later Opal came in. Judging by the bits of twig in her fur and the trail of wet pawprints across the floor, she had been exploring the garden, and now she started to tell them all about it in a non-stop series of wowls and squawks and mews.

"God, she's noisy, isn't she?" said Danny.

"Most Siameses are," Rhoda defended. "I call it talkative."

He raised his eyebrows. "Watch it – you sound like Mrs W again! Hey, Opal, c'mere." He snapped his fingers and was loftily ignored.

"She's picky about her friends," Rhoda told him wickedly. "But if you want to get on the right side of her, sit down and offer her a lap. She loves that."

"OK." Crossing the room, Danny flopped into the old armchair and thumped both hands down on his knees. "Come on then, snooty! Sit!"

Tempted, Opal started towards him.

And stopped, staring at the chair.

"Come on!" Danny coaxed again. "What's the matter, aren't I good enough for you?"

Opal hissed. Her tail fluffed up like a bottle-brush. Then, like lightning, she streaked away and hid behind the cupboard.

"Well, thanks a bunch!" Danny said indignantly. Then he saw Rhoda's face. "And there's no need for you to stare like that, either! Anyone'd think I'd suddenly grown another head!"

"No," said Rhoda quickly. "No, I – er – sorry." She frowned. "It's Opal. That's the second time she's acted like that; she seems to have a thing about the chair. She won't go near it."

"She probably doesn't like the smell," Danny suggested.

"That's what Mum said. Only. . ." Rhoda paused, and Danny prompted, "Only what?"

"Ohh . . . nothing." She was thinking of the dream, but she didn't want to tell Danny about it. He'd only laugh.

Seeing that she wasn't going to say any more, Danny wriggled in the chair and rested his head against the high back. "Hey, this is pretty comfortable!" he said. "I could go to sleep here. Lovely!"

He shut his eyes and made snoring noises.

Ignoring him, Rhoda carried on arranging ornaments. Then suddenly Danny said,

"Aha! Changed your mind, have you?"

"What?"

"Not you – Opal. She's jumped on my lap."

Rhoda looked down and saw the twitching brown tip of Opal's tail protruding from beneath the cupboard. "What are you talking about?" she said. "Opal's here, by my feet."

She turned round in time to see Danny sitting up. His eyes were open again and there was a look of baffled surprise on his face.

"She was here! I felt her land on me, and I heard her purring. . ." Then he stopped as he, too, saw the Siamese's tail. Instantly he was on his feet, scrambling away from the chair and then turning to look at it as though it had abruptly turned into something monstrous.

"Danny?" Rhoda probed.

Danny shook his head. "Must've dozed off." His voice had changed; he sounded defensive. "Yeah – I dozed off, and dreamed it."

"You can't possibly have done," Rhoda said. "Not in that short a time."

"Well, I did, didn't I?" Danny's face was tense and there was an evasive look in his eyes;

a look that told Rhoda he was lying. Something peculiar had happened to Danny just now, and it had scared him so much that he didn't want to face it.

And that made Rhoda wonder if maybe this wasn't the first weird experience he had had. . .

Suddenly Danny made a very obvious show of looking at his watch. "Hey, I'd better go," he said, trying and failing to sound casual. "Got things to do." He looked at her, but furtively. "Sorry I can't help you finish this, but . . . well, you know."

"Yes," said Rhoda meaningfully. "I know *exactly*."

To her disappointment, though, he refused to take the bait but only gave her what was supposed to be a smile. It wasn't convincing.

"Right, then," he said. "See you."

"Sure. See you." *But not until you've got over the fright*, Rhoda added silently to herself. *I'll bet anything on that.*

She heard the door bang as Danny went out, and through the rain-streaked window saw him hurry away to his own house. Noises from upstairs told her that Mum and Dad were moving furniture around in their bedroom. Before they came down, she wanted to try an experiment.

Rhoda moved towards the armchair. Opal gave a grumbling growl as she did so, and a little shiver went through her. It was as if the cat was trying to tell her something. Something about the chair? Well, there was only one way to find out.

She sat down and, as Danny had done, closed her eyes.

Nothing happened. Rhoda waited for nearly two minutes, but there was no sudden sensation of a warm, heavy presence on her lap. At last she opened her eyes again as rationality came back with a vengeance. This was totally daft! The chair wasn't something out of a horror movie – it was just a chair, and Danny hadn't been scared or lying but really had dozed off for a few seconds.

"Trouble with you, Rhoda Mackay," she said out loud, "is that you've got too much imagination and you let it run away with you." It was typical of her to look for a weird answer to a mystery rather than a sensible one, and with a sigh she stood up. There couldn't possibly be anything eerie about the armchair, and if Opal wouldn't go near it, it was simply one of her choosy fads. She'd probably change her mind in a day or two and decide that the chair was Hers, and then they'd never get her off it.

In a way Rhoda was almost disappointed, because the idea of there being something spooky about their new home was quite exciting. But then she recalled the dream again. Spooky thrills were great in books and movies, but she didn't *truly* want them to be real. No one in their right mind would, would they?

She sighed again, and went back to the task of unpacking ornaments.

4

Danny didn't come to the house at all for the next three days. By itself that might have been enough to make Rhoda's suspicions stir again – but in the light of the other things that were happening, Danny was the least of her worries. She didn't even give him a thought. Because too much else was going on.

On the following night, she had the dream again. This time, to her relief, she didn't sleep-walk but simply woke up in bed, feeling very shaken. For a moment she thought she could hear Opal purring on the window ledge, but when she looked towards the moonlit window the Siamese wasn't there. Deciding that it must have been an echo from the nightmare, Rhoda managed to get back to sleep again, and the rest of the night was peaceful.

Then, the next evening, the really unnerving thing happened.

Rhoda and her parents had had quite enough of house-straightening for one day, and were watching television in the sitting-room, with their dinners on their laps. Mum and Dad were on the sofa, while Rhoda sat in the old armchair. Opal still wouldn't come near the chair, so for once Rhoda was able to eat a meal without the Siamese patting her leg with a paw and noisily demanding Her share. When everyone had finished she took the plates out to the kitchen, then returned to settle down and watch what looked as if it might be a good thriller. Dad was half asleep, and Mum kept a vague eye on the screen while she was doing a crossword, and after a time Rhoda began to feel deliciously drowsy. She closed her eyes, though still listening to the film dialogue – then she sensed a presence nearby, and a moment later felt the unmistakable weight of Opal jumping on to her lap.

"Hiya, puss," she said lazily. Opal settled

comfortably, and Rhoda felt pleased that she'd finally got over her sulks and decided to give the chair a try. Eyes still shut, she reached out a hand to stroke the cat's fur.

There was nothing there but her own knees.

Rhoda's eyes started open and she stared at the empty space where Opal should have been. This was insane! She could *feel* the Siamese, as surely and solidly as she could feel herself – yet Opal wasn't anywhere in sight!

Rhoda looked wildly towards the sofa, her mouth opening to blurt to Mum and Dad. Then the sound caught and jammed in her throat as she saw her cat. Opal was on the sofa's middle cushion, wedged between her parents and stretched out to full length with her head on her front paws. She looked lazy and relaxed – but her blue eyes were open, and glaring with a fixed, brilliant stare at Rhoda's legs.

She was watching something. And the invisible weight on Rhoda's lap tensed and shifted, as if that same something was glaring straight back.

With a huge effort, Rhoda managed to get out a single, croaking word. "Mum. . ."

"Mmm?" Mum looked up. She smiled. She

obviously didn't notice anything strange, and suddenly Rhoda couldn't find the words to tell her. Mum would only laugh and say she must have been dreaming, just as Danny had done. Only Rhoda wasn't dreaming. She was wide awake, and the invisible *something* was still there.

"I . . . er. . ." Rhoda fished frantically for anything to say that would get her out of this mad situation. "I'm . . . going to make myself some coffee," she floundered at last. "Anyone else want some?"

Dad didn't answer, and Mum said, "No, thanks." She paused. "I thought you were watching the film?"

"Ohh – it's not as good as I expected. I'll probably take my coffee up to bed – I'm a bit tired."

"Yes, you do look it, I must say. All right, love. Don't forget to clean your teeth afterwards, though."

The idea of doing anything as ordinary as cleaning her teeth made Rhoda want to howl with laughter at that moment. Or perhaps just howl.

What would happen when she stood up? She didn't know, and a large part of her didn't want to find out. But she couldn't sit here like a dummy until *it* decided to go away. So she drew a deep breath, then with a quick, sharp movement got to her feet.

The presence instantly vanished. Rhoda didn't feel it move, but in the space of a single moment it just wasn't there any more. She all but ran out of the room and into the kitchen, where she leaned over the sink feeling giddy with relief at having escaped.

It was still raining heavily; she could hear water pattering on plants in the garden, and trails of it were trickling down the window above the sink. The noise was soothing, calming her jitters a little. Beginning to feel better, she put the kettle on, and while she waited for it to boil she started to think more calmly. Now that the shock was wearing off, she had to admit that the weird incident wasn't *really* frightening. In fact it had been quite pleasant, just like the friendly, comfortable and familiar sensation of having Opal on her knee. If the armchair was haunted – and it was certainly beginning to look that way – then the ghost seemed to be a nice one, not something to strike terror into anybody. The ghost of a cat.

Mrs Wilson's cat? She tried to remember its name, which Danny had mentioned, but it wouldn't come back to mind. She'd have to see Danny again and ask him.

The kettle boiled, and she made her coffee. As she stirred it, a sudden squall flurried against the window, and the kitchen light dipped and flickered violently. Rhoda jumped as if she'd been pricked by a red-hot needle – then, heart bumping, remembered what Danny had said about bad weather and the electricity. A momentary power drop, that was all. She'd get used to it soon enough.

A second squall flung more rain at the window, and again the light flickered. But this time, as the bulb dimmed, Rhoda saw and heard something.

She froze with the spoon in her hand and her mouth open. Eyes – amber eyes, almond-shaped, low down by the floor and *glaring* at her. The image had only been there for a moment, but it was unmistakable. And so was the sound she had heard. A cat's growl.

It could have been Opal, of course. But Opal was in the sitting-room and the door was closed. Besides, Opal's eyes were blue. . .

The light had come back up and everything looked normal again, but suddenly Rhoda didn't want to be alone in the kitchen any more. Grabbing her coffee, she rushed back to the sitting-room. Luckily, her parents didn't notice her jumpiness. Dad seemed to be completely asleep now, and Mum had grown bored with the film and changed channels. Rhoda glanced uneasily at the armchair, but it looked as ordinary as ever, and nothing rose from its depths to leer at her over the arms or back.

" 'Night, then," she said, hoping her voice sounded fairly normal.

" 'Night, love." Mum didn't look up. Opal was on the sofa, with her eyes shut. She rolled over and burped, but she didn't seem worried any more, so Rhoda could only conclude that the ghost – or whatever it was – had gone.

She climbed the steep, twisty stairs, reached the landing and turned towards her bedroom. There wasn't a light on the landing (Dad said the whole house needed rewiring), but at the moment Rhoda preferred that to having lights that dipped and jumped every time the wind blew. The darkness might be creepy, but at least it was *steady*.

She groped her way along until her fingers found the latch of her door. Opening it, she pressed the wall switch inside and the bedroom bulb sprang to life, sending a bright shaft out into the passage.

From the corner of her eye Rhoda saw a small shape whisk quickly across the patch of light and vanish into the shadows.

Her heart gave an enormous leap, and coffee slopped on to the floor as she jumped with the shock. This time she had seen it properly, and it *was* a cat! A plump tabby with a long, fluffy tail almost like a fox's brush. . .

For a few seconds Rhoda stood completely still, until her heart stopped crashing under her ribs. Then, cautiously, she called into the dark.

"Puss? Puss-puss-puss?"

Nothing. If the cat was still there, it wasn't going to show itself again.

"Puss-puss-puss!" she called again, more loudly. From below came Mum's voice: "She's down here, Rho. And you know I don't like you encouraging her into bedrooms!"

Mum thought she was calling to Opal, and hastily Rhoda shouted back, "All right. Sorry."

She peered into the gloom again but still

there was no sign of any movement. Yet she couldn't shake off the feeling that somewhere, not far away but concealed from her, *something* was watching and listening in the dark.

"All right," she said, softly so that Mum wouldn't overhear. "Hide if you want to. But I *did* see you. I know I did."

She went into her bedroom and quietly, thoughtfully, closed the door.

That night, the dream came back for the third time. And Rhoda woke up from it to find herself, again, standing with her hands and nose pressed to the wall of her bedroom.

She was badly scared. She didn't have the least idea what could be causing her to walk in her sleep, and she wanted to tell Mum and ask her advice. But somehow she couldn't bring herself to do that. Mum would worry and whisk her straight off to the doctor, and for reasons which she couldn't properly explain to herself Rhoda did *not* want to get involved in that kind of thing. She decided to wait a while, and see if it happened a third time. If it did, well, then perhaps she *would* talk to Mum. But not yet.

She did work out the answer to one small

puzzle, though; which was the reason why, on both occasions, she had sleepwalked to that particular spot. Working it out, she realized that the wall where she had found herself was in the same place as her bedroom door in their old house. So whatever had taken hold of her last night had been trying to make her go downstairs; and her sleeping mind, not yet used to the new house, had looked for the door in the wrong place.

But why had she wanted to go downstairs at all? It was as if something had called to her, pulled her – and that was really frightening, because if it happened again and she *did* find the door, she could easily fall and break her neck! Rhoda decided that the safest thing to do was tie a piece of string around the latch each night when she went to bed, and make complicated knots that she wouldn't be able to unravel in her sleep. It would be a nuisance in the mornings, or if she needed to go to the loo in the night, but it was better than risking a serious accident.

But though the safeguard made her feel better, it didn't solve the mystery of what was calling to her.

Rhoda avoided the armchair all that day. She wasn't afraid of it – at least that was what she told herself – but it seemed more . . . well, *sensible*, not to invite trouble. In the evening, Mum sat in the chair for a while, but she kept fidgeting uncomfortably and at last declared that she didn't like it, so Dad swapped with her. He wouldn't have noticed if fifty ghosts had been jumping up and down on his lap, so that told Rhoda nothing. But if the invisible presence *had* returned, she herself saw no sign of it.

Before she got into bed, Rhoda tied up the latch of her door as she had resolved. It would take ages to untangle the knotted string tomorrow, but it made her feel a lot more secure. She was tired and fell asleep quickly.

And before long, the dream came creeping back.

It was slightly different this time. Again she found herself drifting down the stairs, but instead of the deafening purring from below, she thought she heard someone crying.

"Mum?" Rhoda whispered concernedly. But somehow she knew that it wasn't Mum. She floated to the foot of the stairs, and as she reached the bottom the door swung open of its own accord.

The crying faded and vanished, as if the volume control on a radio had been turned down. There was no one in the sitting-room – and, as before, it was empty of furniture.

Except for the armchair.

Rhoda found herself moving towards the chair. She didn't want to, but a force outside her control was pulling her, and she knew that it wanted her to sit down. Unable to resist, she lowered herself into the cushioned seat, and waited. Something was going to happen, she knew. But what?

Then the purring began. It came from nowhere and yet everywhere at once, and the sound of it filled the room, rumbling and echoing like thunder. Rhoda looked down.

On her lap was a large tabby cat.

In her dream Rhoda smiled. She reached out and started to stroke the cat's head, and the purring became so loud that it was a roaring in her ears. Louder . . . still louder. . .

And she snapped awake.

To find, to her enormous shock, that she was sitting downstairs, in the armchair, gently stroking the empty air above her knees.

5

Danny said: "It was called Sheba. Why do you want to know?"

Rhoda avoided answering the question. "What did it – she – look like?" she asked.

"I told you before. A great fat tabby, and as bad-tempered as the old girl was." He paused. "It had an amazing tail, though. Really thick and fluffy, just like a fox's. Would've made a great feather-duster."

It was the confirmation Rhoda had been looking for. A fat tabby cat with a splendid tail. Just like the one she had glimpsed on the landing.

"Sheba." She repeated the name thoughtfully. "And you said she died?"

"Yeah." Danny scuffed one foot in the wet grass. "Hey, what's all this interest in Mrs Wilson's cat all of a sudden? It's gone and so has she. Why do you want to know about it?"

Rhoda knew that he really wanted to say, "What the heck's going on?", and the fact that he didn't say it made her wonder if he had a secret or two of his own.

She considered for a few moments, then decided to tell him what had happened, or at least some of it. She *needed* to talk to someone. She just couldn't keep this bottled up for much longer.

"Look," she said cautiously, "if I tell you something, will you promise not to say a word to anyone else?"

Danny shrugged. "Sure."

He was being casual, and she said, "No, I really mean it, Danny. It's important. Above all, I don't want anyone's parents to know."

"OK. I don't talk to mine much anyway. So what's the great mystery?"

"Last night," Rhoda said, "I sleepwalked."

"Yeah? Really?" Danny's eyes lit with

interest. Hooking a leg over the fence, he scrambled across to her side. "What happened? What was it like?"

Rhoda told him the whole tale of her recurring dream – the two occasions when she had woken up facing her bedroom wall, and the third and far more worrying episode last night. She still could hardly believe that she'd carefully untied all the string she'd knotted around her door-latch, but when she had gone shivering back to her room after waking, there it had been, unravelled. She'd even rolled the string up neatly and put it on a shelf before opening the door and going downstairs. And all while she was fast asleep.

Danny whistled through his teeth when he heard that part of the story. "That's quite something!" he said eagerly. "It's amazing you didn't fall and break your neck!"

"Don't tell me!" said Rhoda feelingly. "It was *awful*."

"I'll bet." Then Danny frowned. "But what's it got to do with Mrs W's cat?"

Rhoda sighed. "This is the bit you're not going to believe."

His eyes narrowed. "Try me."

"All right, then. In my dream, just before I woke up, I was sitting in that armchair and there was a cat on my lap." She looked challengingly at him. "A fat tabby with a fluffy tail. Just like your description of Sheba."

There was a long pause. Then Danny shrugged again. "That doesn't mean anything."

"Not by itself, no. But the other night I *saw* that cat. In our house, on the landing. Only when I looked again, there was nothing there."

Another pause. At last Danny said, "Well, it can't have been Sheba, can it?"

"Can't it?"

"Oh, come on! You're not trying to say you think your house is haunted by a cat's ghost, are you?"

Rhoda looked him straight in the eye. "So what scared the hell out of you when you sat in that chair, Danny?"

Danny's mouth opened, shut, opened again. "Nothing," he got out at last.

"Liar," said Rhoda. "Why won't you be honest? I'm not going to laugh at you."

His face reddened and she realized that she'd hit the target. Quickly, before he could

49

recover and think up some excuse to get himself out of trouble, she went on, "I've *seen* Sheba in the house, and I've *felt* her on my lap when I sat in that chair – and so have you, haven't you? Tell me, Danny. Tell the truth!"

The third pause was much longer than either of the others, and she could see Danny struggling with himself. At last he spoke.

"Look," he said, "There's no such things as ghosts, right? Everyone knows that – it's a complete load of rubbish."

"Is it?"

"Course it is! Sleepwalking – that's different; it's real, and if it's happened to you then there's got to be some reason. But it's nothing to do with *ghosts*."

"I think it is," Rhoda persisted.

"And I say it isn't." Danny had a stubborn look on his face now, and she realized that she wasn't going to get the truth out of him this way. She'd have to try another method.

"All right," she said. "I'll prove it to you."

Danny eyed her suspiciously. "How?"

Rhoda didn't know how, but she wasn't about to let that stop her. "You'll see," she said airily.

He snorted. "Yeah, and a pig just flew past! You know what I think? It isn't a ghost that's started you sleepwalking; it's something in your head." He started to climb back over the fence, then paused and looked back. "I'd see the doctor if I were you. You've probably got a brain disease."

"Thanks a bunch!" Rhoda scowled.

He went back indoors, leaving Rhoda feeling annoyed. But Danny's attitude made her all the more determined that she *would* prove the truth to him, and she had an idea. She would try to make friends with the ghost; and if that worked, she'd see if she could persuade it to appear when Danny was around. *That* would show him.

Rhoda looked around at the garden, which was wet and shining after all the rain. What happened to ghosts in the daytime? Did they dissolve away, or was it just that they were less easy to see when the sun was up? Though she couldn't explain it, she had a funny feeling that the unearthly cat was somewhere around, though invisible, and she said softly, "Sheba . . . I want to be your friend. I'm not frightened of you. Please come back. Come to me again."

Only silence answered her. Sheba didn't appear.

But Rhoda believed that she *would* be back. Very soon.

The best way to make friends with a ghost, Rhoda decided, was to encourage it in any and every way that she could. But she certainly hadn't bargained for the effect that her efforts were going to have.

She began by sitting in the armchair as often as she could. Every evening she plonked herself in it, and in the daytime she kept finding excuses for a few minutes' "rest". Mum said she was hogging the chair and Dad teased her about getting old and lazy, but Rhoda didn't care. Because the plan was starting to work.

Sheba was cautious, and more often than not, at first, nothing at all happened when Rhoda sat in the armchair. But little by little the ghost started to get bolder. Soon, Rhoda only had to close her eyes in order to feel the soft, warm pressure on her lap. Then it happened when her eyes were open, too. And after a few days she began sometimes to hear purring. It wasn't Opal; Opal's purr sounded completely different, and besides, this happened when Opal wasn't even in the room. It was Sheba; Rhoda had no doubt of it. Slowly, gradually, she and the spirit of the cat were becoming friends. Even Opal had calmed down. She still wouldn't go near the armchair, and now and then as she passed it she would lay her ears back and hiss and swear, as if she could see something that human eyes couldn't. But apart from that, she seemed to accept Sheba's presence with a kind of sulky tolerance.

To Rhoda, the fact that there was an amiable ghost in the house was wonderful and thrilling. She'd often fantasized about something like this – just as she fantasized about going back into the past – but she hadn't imagined that it could ever really happen to her. She would have loved to tell someone about it and share the secret. Mum and Dad, though, were out of the question. For a start they wouldn't have believed her; and even if they did, Mum would be terrified by the thought of anything spooky. She'd want to call in an exorcist or whatever, to "get rid of it". No, Rhoda thought; she'd just have to be patient, and wait for the right moment to prove the truth to Danny.

She hadn't caught herself sleepwalking again. The dreams had stopped, too, which was a relief. But then, Rhoda had what she could only think of as another kind of dream. A waking dream.

She was in the garden watching Opal, who had discovered the old apple tree and was happily climbing it, squawking and meowling as if to say, "Look at me, aren't I clever," as she scrambled among the branches. The sun was shining at last, and Rhoda was listening to Opal's noisy comments and thinking how great it was that there was more than a week of the Easter holidays still left. Then suddenly, at the edge of her vision, she glimpsed a movement in the grass.

She turned her head, and was just in time to see a fluffy, tabby tail disappearing into the undergrowth.

"Sheba. . .?" Rhoda's eyes widened in astonishment. The grass rustled as if something had disturbed it, then was still again, and cautiously Rhoda began to move towards the spot where the tail had vanished. She hardly dared believe that Sheba had appeared in broad daylight – but that tail was so distinctive;

there surely couldn't be another cat, a living cat, with one like it?

She poked around in the grass but found nothing. Opal had stopped squawking; she was crouching on a branch and watching Rhoda very intently. Then she growled. A prickling sensation crawled up Rhoda's spine. And suddenly she had the unshakeable feeling that there was someone – or something – behind her.

Very slowly she straightened up and turned round. . .

Five tabby cats were walking in single file across the garden. But they weren't flesh-and-blood animals; they were semi-transparent, the grass and bushes visible through them like a film projected on to a different background.

Rhoda's jaw dropped and, stunned, she could only stare dumbly as the cats walked on. Then the last cat in the line paused, turned its head and looked straight at her. It was Sheba – and as she stared into Rhoda's eyes, the scene wavered and changed and suddenly the garden was different. Instead of the riotously over-grown tangle there was a neat lawn, well-tended plants, much smaller shrubs. . .

And someone else was there.

Rhoda only had time for one glimpse before, with a jolt, everything returned to normal. The cats vanished. The garden was back the way it had been. But the human figure she had seen in that moment was fixed in her mind – and she had seen it before. A tall, thin woman, wearing old-fashioned clothes.

She was the woman in the old photo that Rhoda had found upstairs.

Rhoda stood very still, gazing at the place where the figure had briefly appeared. Was the thin woman a ghost, too? Without knowing why, Rhoda had the strangest feeling that she wasn't. It was more as if . . . she racked her brain, trying to make sense of everything . . . as if time had slipped momentarily, and she had peeked at a scene from the past. Just like her fantasies.

Only this time, it had been real.

A plaintive cry from the apple tree snapped her back to earth and she saw Opal coming down backwards, gripping with her claws and making a great fuss about it. Dropping to the ground, the Siamese ran to Rhoda and began to rub around her legs. She seemed to be trying to say something, and Rhoda sighed.

"I know, Opie. I saw them, too. But I don't know what it means, any more than you do."

Why *five* cats? Until now, there had only been signs of one. And Sheba had never appeared in daylight before. What did they want? What were they trying to *tell* her?

She looked around the garden, but everything was completely normal again. No cats, no visions. The sun had gone behind a cloud, and suddenly it felt cold.

Rhoda shivered and went indoors. She didn't see the curtain twitch at the window of the house next door. And she didn't see Danny, his face pale and his eyes worried, turn away from the window and hurry upstairs to his room.

6

"It was very peculiar," Mum said, her voice muffled through the sitting-room door. "I'd have *sworn* I felt her jump on my lap, but when I looked she wasn't there."

Rhoda had been about to come in from the kitchen, but as she heard this she froze with her hand half-way to the latch.

Dad said, "Pins and needles, probably. You'd been sitting in one place for too long."

"I'd only been there for two minutes," said Mum.

"Well, maybe Opal jumped on and jumped off again before you could see her." Dad

58

sounded distracted; he was trying to put up a curtain rail and couldn't get it straight.

Mum muttered something about nobody ever taking any interest in anything she said, and Rhoda jumped quickly back from the door as she heard footsteps approaching on the other side.

"Oh, there you are," said Mum, coming in. "We're almost out of milk – go to the village shop and get me some, would you?" She gave Rhoda a pound coin, then hesitated. "Rho. . ."

"Yes?" Rhoda looked back uneasily. She had a feeling she knew what was coming.

"That old armchair," said Mum. "You haven't noticed anything . . . strange about it, have you?"

"Strange?" Rhoda echoed, hoping that her face wasn't giving her away. "Er . . . what sort of strange?"

Mum looked almost embarrassed. "I mean, when you've sat in it, you haven't . . . *felt* anything?"

"No," Rhoda lied, pretending to be puzzled.

"Oh," said Mum. "All right. I just wondered. . ." She was frowning, but before she could ask any more questions Rhoda said, "I'll go to the shop, then," and made her escape.

So the armchair hauntings had started happening to Mum, too. Hurrying down the garden path, Rhoda felt worried. The last thing she wanted was Mum getting involved; if she realized that there was a ghost in the house she'd completely freak, and that would ruin everything. If only Danny would talk to her! She was sure he knew more about Sheba than he would admit, and she badly wanted his help. Rhoda was certain that the ghostly cat – or cats – weren't just hanging around for no reason. They had a *purpose*. They were trying to *tell* her something. But without some clues, she didn't know how to find out what that something was.

She peered towards the house next door, but there was no sign of Danny. He was hiding from her, she was sure of it. Well, he couldn't hide for ever, could he? She'd said she would prove to him that Sheba was real, so she'd just have to find a way to do it. Somehow. *Somehow*.

* * *

Sheba came back again that evening. Rhoda felt her almost as soon as she sat down in the armchair, and a few minutes later, like a faint echo, she heard purring. And Opal wasn't in the room.

The TV was on; Dad was watching the news and Mum was going round the house looking for something that she'd "Only put down half a minute ago, I *know* I did." Then suddenly, half-way across the floor, Mum stopped.

"Where's Opal?" she said.

Rhoda tensed and pretended not to have heard.

"She's on your window ledge, Rho," Mum went on. "I just saw her. But. . ." She was beginning to look uneasy.

Still Rhoda didn't answer. She was horribly aware that Mum had come closer and was staring at her. Or rather, at the armchair.

"If I didn't know better," Mum said, very slowly, "I'd think there was another cat in this house. . ."

Dad, who wasn't really listening, said, "What's that? We don't want another cat!" and Rhoda thought desperately, *Sheba, Mum can hear you! Be quiet; oh please, be quiet!*

Mum moved away from the chair. She was still looking at it, but she didn't say anything else. Instead, she turned and went quickly into the kitchen. Rhoda breathed a huge sigh of relief. And the warm, invisible weight on her lap shifted and settled itself more comfortably, as the purring faded into silence.

Later, in her room, Rhoda took the cat pictures that Mrs Wilson had left behind from her drawer. She had thrown away the ones that were too tatty to be rescued, but now she spread the others out on her duvet and sat thoughtfully looking at them. She had been going to parcel them all up and send them to Mrs Wilson at the home; after what had happened in the last couple of days, though, she was glad she hadn't. And as she studied the pictures, Rhoda's gaze kept being drawn to the old black-and-white snapshot of the plump tabby cat with the old-fashioned woman in the background.

She was fairly sure that the woman in the photo was Mrs Wilson herself. A much younger Mrs Wilson, of course, which suggested that the vision Rhoda had had in the garden today was a kind of time-slip.

And, somehow, it had all been Sheba's doing.

Rhoda was convinced that the clue she so desperately needed lay in this old photo. But what did it *mean*? The cat in the picture couldn't be Sheba; it had been taken far too long ago for that to be possible. Hadn't Danny said something about Mrs Wilson always having cats? Maybe this was one of her previous pets. One of the other ghosts she had seen earlier. . .?

With a sigh Rhoda scooped up the pictures and put them back in the drawer. She wasn't going to find any answers just by sitting here and staring. Danny, and Sheba. *They* were the only ones who could help her.

So she just had to find a way to persuade them.

That night, Rhoda walked in her sleep yet again.

The dream began in the same way as before; Rhoda was floating down the stairs towards the sitting-room door, while the purring thrummed loudly below. Then, unexpectedly, another sound broke in. A human voice – no, *two* voices. A man and a woman, and it sounded as if they were arguing. Rhoda tried to make out what was being said – or rather shouted – but the quarrel was too muffled for any words to be audible.

Rhoda wanted to rush into the sitting-room and see who was there. But when she struggled to move faster, the dream wouldn't let her. It had control over her, and she was powerless to fight it; all she could do was wait as, agonizingly slowly, she drifted to the foot of the stairs. The sitting-room door swung open – and instantly the voices stopped, and Rhoda was confronted by an empty room.

She knew vaguely that she should have been disappointed, but the dream was still controlling her and she felt only a slight sense of annoyance as she floated towards the armchair. The purring grew louder as she sat down, and moments later there was Sheba, jumping on to her lap and curling up there. Rhoda began to stroke the tabby cat, and crooned to her: "There, Sheba, beautiful Sheba; aren't you a lovely puss. . ."

"Rhoda. . .?" said a familiar voice, from behind her.

Rhoda smiled in her dream but didn't bother to look round. "Hello, Mum. Look, here's Sheba."

"*Rhoda!*"

There was an enormous jolt that seemed to shake Rhoda from head to toes. The moonlit scene turned upside-down, then snapped out of existence as she lurched awake—

She was downstairs again, sitting in the armchair, stroking a cat that wasn't there. And in front of her, staring at her with a look of disbelieving horror, was Mum.

It was Rhoda's sheer bad luck that Mum had woken up after a funny dream, and heard a voice downstairs. Then just as she was about to shake Dad and hiss that there were burglars in the house, she had realized that the voice was Rhoda's.

Mum guessed that one of two things was going on. Either there was something wrong with Opal, and Rhoda was talking to her, or she was making a secret telephone call to someone. Either way Mum wanted to know what was going on, so she tiptoed downstairs to investigate. When she opened the door, there was Rhoda, sitting in the old armchair with her hands making stroking movements, and talking to herself.

Mum hadn't stopped to think; she'd just called out, and her shout of alarm broke the sleepwalking spell. Now, though, she wasn't going to be satisfied until Rhoda had answered some questions. And though Rhoda didn't want to confess, the story of the dream and the sleepwalking eventually came out.

Mum was worried and angry at the same time. She gave Rhoda a lecture of the "why-didn't-you-tell-me-this-was-going-on" variety, and Rhoda could only listen guiltily and say, yes, she *had* been stupid and she *could* have hurt herself, and if it ever happened again she promised *faithfully* that she'd tell Mum straight away. She had managed to keep part of her secret, the part about the armchair hauntings. Or so she thought.

But then Mum dropped the real bombshell.

"All right, Rho," she said, calming down at last. "I won't go on at you any more, and I won't tell Dad, and I won't make you see the doctor. But you've got to answer one more question – and you'd better tell me the truth!"

Rhoda started to feel uneasy. "What question?" she said cautiously.

"That chair." Mum pointed to the armchair, where Rhoda was still sitting. "There's something funny about it. And I think you know what it is."

On Rhoda's lap, a soft weight stirred. Oh, yes; Sheba was still there. Rhoda had been aware of her from the moment she woke up. Sheba was listening. And Rhoda had the nasty feeling that she didn't like what she was hearing.

She said, "Mum, leave it, can't you? The chair's all right, and—"

"It is *not* all right!" Mum interrupted angrily. "Don't think I haven't noticed, Rhoda. The purring when Opal isn't in the room. The surprised look on your face when you're sitting there sometimes, as if a cat had just jumped on your lap. The—"

"Mum. . ." Rhoda pleaded.

But Mum wasn't going to be put off. "*No*," she said fiercely. "Don't pretend, and don't lie! This chair's haunted, isn't it?" She paused, almost glaring at Rhoda. "*Isn't it?*".

Sheba's invisible weight moved again,

tensing. And a soft, low growl vibrated in the air.

It was *such* a soft sound that it was almost inaudible. But Mum heard it. She started violently, her face turning greyish-white, and desperately Rhoda said,

"Mum, there's nothing to be scared of! It isn't an evil ghost, it isn't dangerous, it's only—"

"Not *dangerous*?" Mum's voice shot up the scale alarmingly. "When you've been walking in your sleep, coming down those steep stairs and sitting here *talking* to it?"

"But *Mum*—"

"Don't 'But Mum' me! I'm not having these horrible things happening in my house! I won't *tolerate* it! I don't know what you've done to start all this, but it's going to stop, do you hear me?" Suddenly she jumped to her feet and grabbed Rhoda's arm. "Get up, come on!"

Rhoda felt Sheba leap away as Mum hauled her out of the armchair. Grasping hold of the chair, Mum started to heave it across the floor towards the kitchen.

"What are you doing?" Rhoda cried.

"I'm not having this thing in the house a

moment longer! It's going outside, and it'll stay there until I've decided what to do about it!"

Rhoda wanted to shout, *You can't, you mustn't, it's only Sheba and this isn't fair!* But Mum's stubborn expression told her that it was no use to protest. Mum wouldn't even listen, let alone see reason. She had reached the kitchen now and was dragging the chair with her. "Open the back door," she demanded.

Rhoda couldn't argue. Miserably she unlocked the door and pulled it open. Mum and the chair disappeared outside; there was some grunting, then a thump, and Mum came back indoors again.

"Right," she said grimly. "There it stays. Don't you touch it, Rhoda. Don't you dare even go *near* it!"

Rhoda was close to tears. "What are you going to do with it?" she asked.

"I'll think about that in the morning. Right now, I'm seeing you back to bed, and then I'm going to try and get some sleep!" She locked the door again. "It's lucky for you that your father's a heavy sleeper."

"Dad won't want to get rid of the chair,"

Rhoda said, clutching at straws. "He likes it!"

"Never you mind about Dad. Go to bed, Rho. Go on. *Now*."

There was nothing Rhoda could do. Shoulders sagging in defeat, and with Mum right behind her, she trailed to the stairs. Foot on the first step, she looked back to the empty space where the armchair had stood. The room looked strangely bare without it. Bare . . . and suddenly very unfriendly.

"Rho. . ." said Mum warningly.

Without a word, Rhoda started to climb the staircase. And as the door closed, a patch of shadow flickered on the floor where the chair had been. And a deep-throated, menacing growl echoed softly through the room.

7

In the morning, Dad didn't say anything about the armchair. He must have noticed that it was in the garden, but he didn't mention it once, and when Rhoda tried to bring up the subject she was silenced by an intimidating look from Mum.

When Mum sent her on an errand later, she didn't realize that it was a trick. At the time, there didn't seem to be anything suspicious about it; Mum simply asked her to do some shopping.

And by the time she came back, it was too late.

She saw the smoke as she came up the lane from the village. At first she only wrinkled her nose at the woody, acrid smell and thought that it was the wrong time of the year for bonfires.

But then she realized that the smoke was coming from their own back garden.

The awful realization hit Rhoda, and she ran faster than she'd ever done in her life, pounding up the road, through the gate, down the narrow side passage to the back of the house.

Mum was there, in the garden. She had a rake in her hand, and she was standing guard over a pile of old twigs and branches and dead leaves; all the stuff that Dad had been clearing from the garden. The pile was ablaze.

And in the middle of it, wreathed in merrily crackling flames and already charred and ruined, was Sheba's chair.

"*Mum!*" Rhoda yelled in horror.

Mum turned and looked at her. She didn't say a word, but just smiled a grim, triumphant smile. Then she put down the rake, took the shopping bag from Rhoda's unresisting hand, and went indoors, leaving Rhoda alone in the garden.

Rhoda stood staring blankly at the cheerfully leaping fire. There was nothing at all she could do. She wanted to run after Mum and scream at her, call her names, pummel her with clenched fists; but what was the point? All the screaming in the world couldn't save the chair now.

Feeling too numb even to cry, Rhoda turned desolately away. As she dragged her feet towards the house, the chair's stuffing caught light and went up with a *whoof* of flame.

And echoing the noise of it came another sound. A long, furious, wailing noise that rose above the flames' crackle and then, like the bonfire smoke, went spiralling up and blew away to nothing on the wind.

"Sheba?" Rhoda spun round, half expecting to see the ghostly cat. But there was only the empty garden, with the fire's light reflecting brightly on the bushes and the shed beyond. No Sheba.

But she was there. Rhoda knew it.

And they hadn't heard the last of her.

For the next hour Rhoda and Mum didn't speak to each other, and at last Rhoda couldn't bear the silence any longer. She had to steel herself to go back into the garden, but she needed to know and see the worst for herself.

The bonfire had died down, and the armchair was reduced to a charred and blackened skeleton, sitting forlornly in a heap of smouldering ashes. For a very long time Rhoda just stood staring dejectedly at the remains. She still couldn't cry. She still felt completely numb.

Then a voice said, "So you got rid of it, then?"

Rhoda spun round, to see Danny hovering on the other side of the fence.

"Oh, it's you." At this moment she hated everyone in the world; but she hated him most of all, for being such a coward about Sheba. "Crawled out from under your stone at last, have you?" she added nastily.

Danny's eyes flashed with anger. "Charming! As if it was *my* fault."

"It is your fault!" Rhoda fired back. "If you hadn't—" Then she stopped and turned away. "Oh, forget it." She couldn't truly blame Danny, and abruptly she felt guilty. "Sorry," she added in a mumble. "I'm upset, that's all."

"Over an old chair? Get real, Rhoda!" He hesitated. "It's the one you told me about, is it? The one you reckon was haunted?"

Rhoda scowled and nodded. "Not that you care."

"No, I don't. Why did your mum burn it?"

Something in his tone alerted Rhoda and she looked at him sidelong. *You really want to know, don't you?* she thought. *In fact, you're busting with curiosity.*

"What's it to you?" she asked slyly.

Danny shrugged, trying to appear careless. "Just seems a bit dumb, that's all. You said she liked it."

"Yeah, she did. But something made her change her mind."

Aha! A look of alarm crossed Danny's face, and he wasn't quite quick enough to hide it. Rhoda smiled to herself and said aloud, "If you want to know why Mum burned the chair, you'd better ask her. But I think you've already made a guess. And you're dead right."

Danny's cheeks flushed. He didn't say a word; he just turned on his heel and started to walk away.

Then, half way across the garden he

jumped and said, "Ow!"

He stopped. Rhoda saw him look down, then his face turned pallid and without so much as a glance at her he walked hurriedly on again. As he vanished, she peered at the spot where he had paused. There were no brambles or nettles there; nothing at all that could have caught his leg.

But *something* had obviously scratched him.

So what, Rhoda wondered, could it possibly have been. . .?

She went slowly back to the house and into the sitting room. Opal was there. The Siamese was sitting in the empty space where the armchair had been, and when she saw Rhoda she gave a smug chirrup, as if to say: "Good, *she's* gone and now *I* can have all your attention again!"

"Oh, Opal. . ." Rhoda crouched down and stroked her cat's head. "You needn't have hated Sheba. She wasn't your rival – I still love you best." But now that her chair was gone, would Sheba ever come back? If only Mum hadn't over-reacted. If only she'd *listened*.

Opal purred happily, pushing her head against Rhoda's hand, which was her way of asking for "More, more!" Then abruptly she got up and trotted towards the kitchen, looking back with a hopeful expression.

"All right," Rhoda said. "Just a bit. Though it isn't really food time yet." She stood up, pausing a moment to gaze sadly at the empty space by the hearth. "Sorry, Sheba," she whispered.

She started to turn away.

And something scratched her leg.

"Ouch!" Rhoda yelped. "All *right*, Opal, I'm coming! That's a bad habit of yours, clawing when you don't get what you. . ."

Her voice tailed off. Because Opal was still sitting by the kitchen door.

Rhoda's heart began to thump. She looked down at her leg.

Just above her ankle, red and angry and trickling blood, were the long, clear marks of a cat's claws.

So Sheba hadn't gone after all. And for the rest of that day, Rhoda couldn't shake off the conviction that something was waiting to happen. It was a feeling in the air, an atmosphere, hovering over her wherever she went and

77

whatever she did; and as night fell it seemed to close in like a silent, invisible threat. Nothing else did actually happen. But the weird incident of the scratches had been all too real, and however hard she tried, Rhoda couldn't make her fear go away.

By the time she went to bed she was completely frazzled; jumping at her own shadow, heart leaping with fright at the slightest noise. The wear and tear on her nerves was exhausting, and within minutes of climbing under her duvet she was fast asleep.

But she didn't sleep for long.

It started with the purring. The sound woke Rhoda up, and she started, opening bleary eyes to find that her room was pitch dark. She held her breath apprehensively, listening. It *was* a purr, wasn't it? Not a threatening growl. . .? Yes; she was certain now. It must be Opal then, not Sheba, and Rhoda sighed with relief.

"Hi, Opie," she murmured sleepily. Judging from the direction of the purring, Opal was on the floor by the bed, and Rhoda stuck a hand out from under the duvet, snapping her fingers. "Come on, then, jump up. I won't tell Mum."

She felt Opal spring lightly on to the bed, then came the careful tread of paws moving up towards her head. The purring grew louder. Rhoda felt warm breath on her face, and in the gloom saw the silhouettes of two pointed ears. For a moment Opal stood still, looking at her.

Then with a savage snarl a dark shape launched itself, claws flashing, straight for Rhoda's eyes.

Rhoda gave a yell that was muffled by the duvet. Pure instinct made her roll sideways as the claws slashed at her, and she fell out of bed, landing with a thud on the floor. Scrabbling and flailing, she grabbed the edge of her bedside table; her fingers groped for the lamp, pressed the switch, and as the bulb came on she was just in time to glimpse something leaping from the bed and streaking across the floor to the window ledge. The curtains flapped as if a wind had blown them – and the shape was gone.

On hands and knees, mouth open and gaping in shock, Rhoda stared at the window as the curtains settled and hung limp again. Her heart was thundering like a sledgehammer and for a few moments she really and truly thought she was going to be sick from sheer fright. Then the feeling faded, and in its place came a sense of slow, creeping shock.

Sheba. She had pretended to be Opal, lulling Rhoda into a false sense of security with her purring, then had attacked her in her own bed! Shakily, Rhoda got to her feet and stumbled over to the window, wrenching back the curtains. There was no sign of Sheba, of course. And the window was shut. She must have vanished straight through it, as if the glass didn't exist.

Suddenly from below came a piercing howl – the unmistakable sound of an angry Siamese cat.

"Opal!" Rhoda dived for the door. The fracas in her bedroom hadn't woken Mum or Dad yet, but Opal's howling soon would. She scrambled downstairs, trying desperately to be quiet, and ran into the sitting-room. No Opal. Rhoda hurried to the kitchen, and as soon as she switched the light on she saw the Siamese. Opal was pacing up and down in front of the back door, growling, her tail lashing wildly. As Rhoda ran to her she howled again, and her message was clear: "Let me out, let me OUT!"

"No, Opal, be quiet!" Rhoda picked up the

cat. Opal struggled, desperate to get out into the garden, but Rhoda held on tightly. No *way* was she going to open the back door; not with Sheba maybe lurking right outside, lying in wait. . .

"No!" she told Opal again. As if she understood that she wasn't going to get her way, the Siamese quietened, though rumbling complaints still vibrated in her throat. Her sides heaved angrily and her tail thwacked against Rhoda's face; ignoring it, Rhoda took a cautious step towards the door, listening hard. No sound out there. . . At last she let out her pent breath and put Opal down on the floor, where she slunk over to the far corner and sat sulking by the cooker.

Rhoda looked at her. "It *was* Sheba," she whispered. "You sensed her, didn't you?"

Opal's answer was a throaty, ominous hiss, which was all the confirmation Rhoda needed. She listened a moment longer, then retreated from the kitchen, switched off the kitchen light and went quietly but quickly back up the stairs, carrying Opal with her. She didn't think Sheba would return, but she'd feel a lot happier – and safer – to have the Siamese for company for the rest of the night.

As for tomorrow. . . Well, she didn't know what she could do. But one thing was certain. Mum had made a very big mistake – for instead of getting rid of Sheba, the destruction of the old armchair had triggered her fury, and she was out for revenge. Something had to be done, before the ghostly cat's anger got right out of hand.

Before it got downright *dangerous*.

8

Within another day, it was obvious that Sheba had just one target for her fury – Rhoda. It didn't seem to matter that the loss of the chair wasn't Rhoda's fault; Sheba had decided to take it out on her, and that was that.

By the following evening, Rhoda didn't dare approach the spot in the sitting-room where the chair had stood. If she did, if she even tried, Sheba attacked her. And the incredible thing was that, though Sheba was a ghost, her attacks were real. She scratched Rhoda's legs. She bit Rhoda's ankles. She snarled and hissed – though never, now, when there was anyone else in the room. And when Rhoda sat on the sofa in the evening (as far away as she could get from the hearth), she could feel the cat's malevolent, invisible presence by the fireplace, just waiting for her next chance to strike.

What had started as a bit of fun was turning into a nightmare. All Rhoda's fanciful and romantic ideas about the house's "nice" ghost had gone horribly wrong, and she didn't know what to do. She couldn't talk to Mum or Dad, and Danny was no use; he was avoiding her again. Could she somehow reason with Sheba? Out of Mum and Dad's hearing she tried it, whispering explanations, pleas, even threats (though what on Earth *could* you threaten to do to a ghost?). But Sheba wasn't interested.

Rhoda made her last effort just before she went to bed. Wanting a late-night biscuit, she walked into the kitchen – and Sheba was waiting for her behind the door. Rhoda sensed the baleful presence a split second before the tabby cat pounced, but she had no time to get out of the way. She yelped as a red-hot pain seared down her shin, and from the sitting-room Mum called, "Rho? Whatever's going on out there?"

"Nothing, Mum," Rhoda lied, hopping on

one leg and clutching the other. "I stubbed my toe, that's all."

She glared round the kitchen. Sheba was under the table; she could feel the invisible stare boring into her. Through clenched teeth she hissed, "Now, *listen*, you! I've had just about all I can take, and it's got to *stop*! For the last time, it's not my fault that your chair got burned, and it isn't fair to keep taking it out on me! *Do you understand?*"

No response. Unless that small, gurgling noise wasn't the water-pipes but something else. . .

"*Please*, Sheba," Rhoda went on more reasonably. "I'm your friend, not your enemy. Stop attacking me. Look, if you stop then I'll try to find you another chair, all right? Is that a deal?"

Was the ghost still there? Suddenly Rhoda wasn't sure; the concentrated patch of fury under the table seemed to have faded. *Oh, great*, she thought. *Talk to yourself, Rhoda, why don't you?*

"Sheba?" she probed. "Sheba!"

Nothing. Rhoda bent down to peer beneath the table-top. And as she did so, the door opened and Mum came in.

"Lost something?" she enquired.

Caught by surprise, Rhoda floundered. "Oh – er, no . . . I mean, yes, I dropped my . . . um . . . anyway, I've got it now, so that's all right."

Mum gave her a suspicious look. "Are you feeling OK, Rho? I thought I heard you talking to yourself."

"Was I? Oh . . . right. I was thinking aloud, I expect." Rhoda smiled pallidly. "Where are the biscuits?"

"In the usual place, in the cupboard." Mum was still looking hard at her. "Rho, are you *sure* you—"

She didn't get any further, because from upstairs came an almighty crash.

Mum jumped and said, "What the—" but Rhoda was already out of the kitchen and pounding up the stairs. She knew, she just *knew*, that the noise had come from her bedroom. And she knew, too, who was responsible.

She burst into her room and slammed the light on. Mum and Dad, puffing up behind her, found her standing in the doorway, staring at the contents of her dressing-table top which lay scattered all over the floor. Tangled jewellery, scrunched-up magazines, spilled talc, a bottle of Cologne with the stopper out. . . And in the middle of the wreckage, smashed to pieces, was Rhoda's Art Deco statuette of a Siamese cat. It was – or had been – her most prized possession.

Which was exactly why Sheba had targeted it.

"Oh, Rho!" said Mum sympathetically. "What a shame!"

"It must have been a gust of wind," Dad added. "The window's open, look." He went to shut it, while Rhoda still stood looking silently at the mess.

"I'll help you clear up, love," Mum soothed. "You never know; maybe we can glue the statue back together."

Rhoda shook her head. "No," she said. "I don't think so." There was a catch in her voice; Mum thought it was tearfulness, but it wasn't anything of the kind. Rhoda wasn't tearful. She was *livid*.

"I'll sort it out," she went on. "Honestly; I'd rather do it on my own."

"Well, if you're sure. . .?"

"Yes. I am."

To her relief they didn't argue but went downstairs and left her alone. She shut the door, then, ignoring the mess, grabbed her retro-psychedelic umbrella from her wardrobe and strode to the bed. Sheba was under there. Rhoda had been aware of her from the moment she ran in, and now she could almost physically *feel* the cat gloating. Her mouth set in a hard line. Sheba was about to get a surprise!

Taking a good grip on the umbrella, she shoved it under the bed like a fencer lunging at her opponent. She didn't know quite what she expected to happen. A ghostly squawk or snarl, perhaps; or a blurred glimpse of something whirling away. But there was no reaction whatsoever.

Surprised and indignant, Rhoda swished the brolly from side to side, but still it had no effect. Sheba must have gone! But she'd have *sworn* the little wretch was still there. . .

She dropped to knees and elbows and peered under the bed. For a few moments she couldn't see anything at all. Then, suddenly, two pinpoints of amber light appeared. They swelled, enlarged, turned into eyes. . .

"*AAAH!*" Rhoda only just rolled out of the way in time as Sheba's ghostly shape hurtled like a rocket from under the bed. A *whoosh* of ice-cold air rushed over her – then a pain like fifty jabbing needles shot through her left foot, and the cat vanished.

Rhoda sat up, her mouth working like a fish's but no sound coming out. Her foot had a semi-circle of red teeth marks in it; they stung ferociously and she rubbed hard at her skin. Then from outside the door came a thump, as if something had thrown itself against the wood, and she heard Opal's unmistakable *wowl*.

Rhoda scrambled up, limped to the door and opened it. Opal tore in with ears flat and tail bristling; she charged round the room as if looking for something, and finally jumped on to the sill, where she stared out of the window and hissed threats.

Rhoda went to join her. It was pitch dark outside and she couldn't see anything. But she knew Sheba was out there somewhere.

And she knew that, before long, she'd be back.

* * *

Rhoda lay nervously awake for most of that night, and by morning she felt physically and mentally exhausted. But one good thing came out of her sleeplessness, because by the time dawn broke, she had come up with the bones of an idea.

There had to be a reason for Sheba's fury at the destruction of the armchair. All right; maybe she had looked on it as "hers", the way Opal did with some pieces of furniture. But surely that alone couldn't explain the violent change in her behaviour? It wasn't as if she needed the chair in order to manifest; her attacks had proved that! So why was she so angry?

Rhoda believed she had an answer. She had been certain from the start that Sheba was trying to tell her something, get some mysterious message across. What, then, if the chair was a vital part of that message? She couldn't imagine how they could be connected, but it made a weird kind of sense. If her theory was right, there was only one thing to be done. And next time Mum went out and left her to herself, she was determined to do it.

Strangely, there were no spooky assaults that morning. Sheba was around, for on several occasions Rhoda heard faint little tell-tale sounds when Opal was nowhere in sight. But she didn't attack.

After lunch, Mum announced that she was going into the town ten miles away to do what she called some "proper" shopping. Rhoda could hardly believe her luck, and as soon as Mum's car was out of sight she ran into the garden.

Dad hadn't yet cleared the remains of the bonfire away. Mum had been nagging him about it, but he'd said that what with work and the house to get straight he didn't have time to worry about garden mess as well, and as Mum had made the bonfire he didn't see why she couldn't clear it up herself. Well, Rhoda thought, grabbing old gloves and a rake and shovel from the shed, Mum would have a nice surprise when she came back. Because *she* was going to clear the bonfire.

And she was going to rescue the remains of the chair.

Opal, ever curious, followed her to the end of the garden, and sat watching interestedly as she set about her task. Although the chair's upholstery had burned and the wood was badly charred, the frame was just about intact, with springs sticking forlornly out at angles from the seat. Grunting and puffing, Rhoda started to heave it out of the debris. It was a struggle, because the chair was heavy, and soon Rhoda was coughing as well, as clouds of ash rose around her. But at last she hauled it clear and, red-faced and grubby, turned to look around the garden for a suitable hiding place where Mum wouldn't find it.

Ah! Those bushes, over beyond the apple tree. Dad said he was going to cut them down and make a compost heap there, but knowing Dad, he wouldn't get round to it till Doomsday. Ideal.

Rhoda took a deep breath, rubbed her dirty face with an even dirtier hand, and dragged the burned-out armchair towards the bushes. Opal still watched her. And so, from the house next door, did someone else. Danny didn't know why Rhoda was rescuing and hiding the chair. He didn't *want* to know, and he certainly wasn't going to offer to help her. But he gazed from his bedroom window.

And he shivered.

9

The rest of the day passed without any more trouble from Sheba.

Rhoda was in her parents' good books for clearing up the bonfire mess, and to her relief Mum didn't even ask what she'd done with the remains of the armchair. The fact that it had gone was apparently enough.

Rhoda went to bed early, taking Opal with her. The last thing she saw before turning off her light was the Siamese's long, sleek form sprawled comfortably on the window ledge. Good. If Sheba tried another night attack, she'd be in for a surprise this time.

Rhoda slept until three o'clock in the morning. Then, again, a noise disturbed her.

She woke – and froze, fear crawling like spiders down her spine as she realized that the sound was that of a cat growling. *There was something on the bed with her, she could feel it*— Panic rose, and Rhoda stifled a scream, hunching up in terror, expecting the flying leap, the savage clawing. . .

Then close to her ear came a soft but distinct Siamese *wowl*.

"Opie. . . ?" Rhoda sat up with a flurry, and reached out to see, in bright moonlight, Opal standing on the bed. The cat's body was rigid and trembling; but she was trembling with excitement rather than fear. Her ears were pricked forward and her nose was pointing towards the door; as Rhoda touched her she *wowl*ed again.

"What is it, Opie?" Uneasily Rhoda peered into the silver-grey gloom. But whatever it was that Opal had seen or heard, her human senses couldn't detect it.

The Siamese wriggled suddenly in her grasp. Rhoda made a grab but Opal evaded her, jumped down, and she heard her paws padding across the floor. Then from the door came the sound of scratching.

Cautious but curious, Rhoda slid out of bed. She lifted the latch, and before the door had swung back more than a few centimetres Opal squeezed through and vanished silently along the landing.

"Opal, come back!" But Rhoda didn't dare raise her voice above a whisper for fear of waking her parents, and the Siamese took no notice. She was heading for the stairs, and in the dim light Rhoda saw her start down them. Moments later she heard scratching again, on the sitting-room door this time. Then Opal yowled impatiently.

"Oh, *blast!*" Rhoda's nervousness collapsed into something much more practical. Opal was just being a pest; she wanted her food dish or her litter tray, and that meant she'd squawk and fuss until someone came to let her through to the kitchen. Thinking sourly that this was getting to be a habit, Rhoda tiptoed along the passage and began to descend the stairs, trying to remember which ones creaked and avoid treading on them if possible. Below, Opal's eyes gleamed at her like sapphires and she yowled again.

"*Shh!*" Rhoda warned. "I'm coming; don't be so impa—"

The words broke off. In the sitting-room, two voices were arguing.

Rhoda's mind flashed back to her recurring dream, and the night when Mum had found her sitting in the armchair and talking to the invisible Sheba. But this time she wasn't dreaming. She was wide awake – and those voices were *real*!

Rhoda all but hurled herself down the last four stairs, and burst into the sitting-room.

The room was peacefully normal – and silent. Each piece of furniture was in its usual place; except for the armchair of course. There was nobody there. But Rhoda's ears caught a faint echo of the voices fading away.

She stood with her hand still on the door latch, staring bewilderedly at the calm scene. What had *happened*? Had she truly heard those voices, or had she imagined them? They had sounded so clear; she had almost – though not quite – been able to make out what they were saying. Now though, it all seemed impossible. . .

Suddenly, from the kitchen, came a cry. It

was Opal; she must have run in there, and now she was meowing loudly, very agitated about something. Shaking her head in confusion, Rhoda went after her and found her, again, by the back door, pacing up and down in the same way as she'd done before. She was frantic to go out. *Why?* There had to be a connection with the voices!

Rhoda opened the door, and Opal rocketed through it and away down the garden. Rhoda hurried out after her, wincing at the cold of the ground under her bare feet. The moon was full in a clear sky, drenching the garden with a spectral, silvery glow that drained all the colour away, like an old black-and-white photo.

Old photos. . . A feeling that was half fear and half excitement clutched at Rhoda's stomach. She could see Opal, a small, pale blur in the moonlight. The Siamese was heading for the far end of the garden. She passed the apple tree, and ran on towards the bushes.

Straight towards the place where the armchair was hidden.

In that moment Rhoda knew what she had to do. It was crazy, *totally* crazy, but a rush of intuition had hit her like a slap in the face and the next thing she knew, she was running down the garden after Opal.

The cat reached the bushes before she did, and as she floundered through the undergrowth in pursuit Rhoda heard her growling on a strange, high-pitched note. The bushes weren't in full leaf yet, so enough moonlight filtered through the branches to show the burned-out chair, pushed between two trunks and leaning wonkily. Opal was crouched in front of the chair, still growling excitedly. She was staring at the twisted springs where the seat used to be, and when Rhoda came up behind her she took no notice at all.

Slowly, Rhoda approached the chair. She was remembering her dream again. Something had compelled her to sit in the chair, and that same something was urging her now. *Sit, sit.* . . *It's the only way, you've got to do it, or you'll never find the answer.* . .

She stepped over Opal, who continued to growl, though more softly now. She stood in front of the armchair, then very, very cautiously and carefully lowered herself on to the ruined remains of the seat. The springs dug into her but she hardly noticed. Her pulse was racing, pounding. What was going to happen? Nothing? Or. . .

"Sheba?" She realized with a small shock that it was her own voice speaking the tabby cat's name. And abruptly Opal fell silent. Her blue eyes stared fixedly at Rhoda. At Rhoda's lap. . .

"Sheba? I'm here, Sheba." Rhoda's whisper sounded eerie in the quiet night, and the bushes rustled as though they were answering her. Her mouth was dry; she licked her lips, horribly aware that she was shivering, and not with cold.

"Sheba. . . Come, Sheba. Come to me. . ."

The moonlight seemed to be growing brighter. One patch in particular, directly in front of her, formed an oval like the polished surface of a mirror. So bright she couldn't see the branches behind it; it was blotting them out. That wasn't *possible*. . .

Suddenly the patch of light flared so brilliantly that Rhoda gasped and turned her head away.

When she looked again, the bushes were gone. In their place was a smooth lawn, with the apple tree standing tall and proud in the middle. To either side were well-tended beds, filled with summer flowers.

And under the apple tree's branches stood two figures. They didn't quite look real; they were there, yet at the same time *not* there, as if she was looking at them through the wrong end of a telescope.

Or looking back through a tunnel in time. . . Because one of the figures was the woman in the old photograph.

Her dress was different – more modern – but Rhoda recognized her face immediately. Now, though, instead of smiling, that face was contorted with anger. The other figure confronted her. It was a man, much younger than she was, and wearing flared trousers and a paisley-patterned shirt. His hair was quite long and cut like a bob, and with a shock Rhoda remembered old pictures Mum had gigglingly shown her of Dad, in his teens in the 1970s. His hair and clothes had been just like these. . .

But this young man looked so much like the woman he was confronting that Rhoda knew at once he could only be her son.

Her mind numbed with astonishment and her body rigid in the ruined armchair, Rhoda stared as before her eyes the two people acted out a strange, silent and furious quarrel. It was like watching a flickering movie from the days before the "talkies" – she saw their mouths move as they ranted and shouted at each other, but there was no sound at all; only bitter gestures and clenching fists and stamping feet as the argument became more savage. At last the young man turned away. He stormed off across the lawn, out of Rhoda's view. The woman stood watching, her face twisted with anger and enmity. She shouted something after him. Then she too turned away, and strode with stiff-backed dignity towards the house.

And from one of the flower beds, a tabby cat emerged and followed at her heels.

The scene wavered suddenly and violently, making Rhoda blink. For a moment her vision blurred. When it cleared again, the woman and the lawn and the flower-beds were gone, and the tangled bushes rustled gently in the night breeze.

Then something else emerged from the bushes, and with a new shock Rhoda found herself staring down at the spectral form of Sheba.

The cat came slowly towards her, gazing up

into her eyes. Opal was no longer there – *where is she?* Rhoda's floundering mind asked frantically – but as Sheba approached, the bushes rustled again and more cats appeared. One after another – three, four, five of them; all translucent, shadowy ghosts.

Rhoda couldn't move. She wanted to jump to her feet and run, away from the cats, away from the bushes, away from the garden. But her muscles wouldn't obey. She was frozen in the chair, cornered, trapped. . .

Sheba opened her mouth, and the faintest of mews whispered in Rhoda's ear. Then she tensed her hind legs, and sprang on to Rhoda's lap. Rhoda recoiled in fright, remembering the ferocious attacks – but Sheba didn't attack her. Instead, landing lightly on Rhoda's knees, she curled up and began to purr. The other cats joined in, the sounds rising louder and clearer and more powerfully, until it seemed to Rhoda that the air was filled with the noise they made, thrumming like a distant thunderstorm.

And the purring was almost like words. Words in a rhythm, repeating over and over again:

Help her. . . Help her. . . Help her. . .

"Help her. . . Help her. . ." Though she

didn't know it, Rhoda was adding her own voice to the cats' purring, like a chant. The sound was so hypnotic; she started to sway in the chair, backwards and forwards, backwards and forwards. *Help her. . .*

Without warning a jolt went through her like a small electric shock. She shook her head dazedly – and the cats and their purring were gone. She was alone in the garden, in the moonlight, sitting in the ruined armchair with only the murmuring voice of the wind to break the silence.

Rhoda rose to her feet. She was shaking so much that her legs wouldn't do what she wanted them to, and it was several minutes before she was able to stumble away from the chair and grope through the bushes into the open.

"Opal. . .?" Her voice quavered. "Opal, where are you. . .?"

A meow from overhead made her look up, and she saw Opal balancing on a branch in the apple tree. The Siamese scrambled down and came running to her, and Rhoda crouched in the damp grass.

"Oh, Opie!" She hugged Opal to her. "It was Mrs Wilson, I'm *sure* it was!" And the young man had looked *so* much like her. Yet Mum had said Mrs Wilson had no family.

"Sheba wants us to help Mrs Wilson," she went on, stroking Opal's head. "And it's something to do with the old chair. That's why she was so angry when it was burned. She *needs* us, Opie." As did all the other cats; cats which, Rhoda was certain, must all once have belonged to Mrs Wilson. A line of little ghosts, leading back through time to a mystery buried in the past. . . The armchair was the key. And somehow, Rhoda had to find the door that that key would unlock. It wasn't just a wish now. It was a *need*.

She stood up, realizing for the first time that she was chilled to the marrow. Hardly surprising; the night was cold and she only had pyjamas on.

"Come on, Opal." She smiled down at the Siamese cat, who chirruped in reply. "Let's get some sleep. Then tomorrow, we've got work to do."

She went back to the house, with Opal trotting at her heels.

And in his unlit bedroom, Danny let the curtain fall and went slowly, thoughtfully back to bed.

10

Rhoda was up very early the next morning. She had done a lot of thinking before going back to sleep, and had decided what her first move should be. But to carry it out, she needed help. She had to talk to Danny – and this time, he wasn't going to wriggle out.

Full of determination, she went into the garden and towards the fence that separated them from next door. She was just about to climb over when Danny emerged from the house.

He stood looking at her, and it was such a strange look that Rhoda stopped in mid-movement. For a moment they both stared. Then Danny came to meet her.

Rhoda said, "I want to talk to you."

"Yes," Danny replied. "I sort of . . . hoped you might."

What did *that* mean? Something had changed, Rhoda realized. Danny wasn't being evasive any more; in fact she got the impression that he wanted to talk as much as she did.

Then he said: "Last night . . . I saw you."

Her heart missed a beat. "Wh . . . what do you mean?" she asked cautiously.

"Come on, Rhoda, don't mess around. Last night. In the garden. I *saw* what you did. And I . . . saw what happened."

"You mean. . ." Rhoda licked her lips nervously, then decided to plunge in. "You saw everything change?"

Danny nodded.

"Those two people, arguing?"

Another nod.

"The woman," said Rhoda. "Was it – was she Mrs Wilson?"

Danny stared at the grass. "I don't know for sure," he said, in a very low voice, "but I think

so. Only she was much, much younger. As if
. . . as if I was looking back in time."

Something inside Rhoda seemed to give way
then, an enormous relaxing that was relief and
excitement and delight all together. But she
had to ask one more question.

"Why are you suddenly willing to believe it
now, when you weren't before?" she said.
"Only a couple of days ago you were trying to
tell me it couldn't happen."

"I know. I suppose I didn't want to let on; I
thought maybe you'd . . . that is. . ." Then
Danny sighed. "OK. I was *scared*. Cos – this
stuff about the ghost cat, and seeing the garden
all changed – it happened to me, too. Before
you came."

It was soon after Mrs Wilson went away to
the home, Danny explained. The sky was
clear and there'd been a full moon, like last
night. He was restless, couldn't sleep, and had
been looking out of his bedroom window,
thinking about nothing in particular, when
before his eyes the next-door garden
shimmered and faded and was replaced by the
same scene Rhoda had witnessed. The woman
and the younger man, arguing. The man

walking away. The cats appearing. Then the vision had vanished, and in his room he heard the sound of purring. And, just as had happened to Rhoda, the purring seemed to form words: *Help her. . . Help her. . .*

"I thought I was going nuts," Danny admitted. "We haven't got a cat, never had one, so where the hell was the noise *coming* from?"

"It was Sheba," said Rhoda quietly. "She was trying to make contact with you. Only you wouldn't listen."

He flushed defensively. "Who in their right mind would?"

Rhoda didn't answer that. "What happened then?" She knew there was more.

Danny looked uncomfortable. "Something started . . . scratching me. In the garden sometimes. Only there was never anything there."

"Sheba again. She's done it to me, too."

He glanced up quickly. "Since when?"

"Since Mum burned the armchair." Rhoda paused. "That day you sat in it . . . you *did* feel Sheba jump on your lap, didn't you?"

"Yeah. Yeah, I did. You see . . . Sheba stopped going for me when you moved in. I just thought, great, I'm not going crazy after all, so I can forget it. But then when that arm-chair thing happened. . ." He met her gaze. "You were an easier target, weren't you?"

Rhoda nodded, understanding. "I was in her house. I sat in her chair. So she could get through to me more easily. She's trying to tell us something, Danny, and the chair's important somehow. That's why she got so angry when Mum put it on the bonfire. She thought no one was going to listen any more."

"Like I didn't listen."

"Exactly."

There was a long silence. At last Danny broke it.

"So where do we go from here?"

"We've got to solve the mystery," said Rhoda.

"Fine. But how?"

"I don't know. Though I know where we could start. If you'll help me."

He raised his head. He was still uncertain, she could tell, but there was a flicker of interest in his eyes. "All right," he said eventually. "What do you want to do?"

Rhoda smiled. "I think we should go and see Mrs Wilson."

* * *

Danny's mum knew the name and address of the home where Mrs Wilson lived. She was surprised that they wanted to visit the old lady, but Rhoda used the excuse that she wanted to take some of the old cards and pictures from the house to her. It was only half an hour away by bus, so three hours later Rhoda and Danny set off.

"I feel a right prat," said Danny, looking down at his own neat, ironed clothes. He glanced at Rhoda, who had put on a skirt and gelled her hair back. "And you look one."

"Listen, if we dressed the way we usually do, they wouldn't let us through the door!" Rhoda told him. "You know the saying: it's all in a good cause."

Danny grunted. He was a lot less sure than Rhoda that this plan was a good idea. As he'd pointed out, he *knew* Mrs Wilson, and she wasn't the sort of person to welcome them with a smile and cheerfully answer their questions. Rhoda wasn't daunted, though. She was certain that this was what Sheba wanted her to do – and she believed that it would work.

The home was called The Glebe, and was a

big Victorian house set back behind wrought-iron gates. Rhododendron bushes lined the drive, and there was a large garden on the far side. From the entrance hall, which was wood panelled and smelled of polish and mashed potatoes, they followed a sign to the Matron's office and knocked on the door.

Matron was surprised when they asked to see Mrs Wilson. Rhoda had the impression that the old lady didn't get any visitors, but she produced the pictures and Matron smiled.

"Well, I'm sure she'll be very pleased to have them. She's in the residents' lounge at the moment. I'll get someone to show you the way."

Rhoda and Danny followed a soft-shoed carer down a long corridor and into a big, sunny room with armchairs all around its edge. Mrs Wilson was sitting by a window, reading a magazine. She had white, tightly-curled hair and pink-framed glasses, and her mouth looked as if it was permanently turned down at the corners. Seeing Danny, she scowled and said,

"What are *you* doing here?"

It wasn't exactly a good start, but Rhoda plunged in.

"How do you do, Mrs Wilson?" she said in her politest voice. "My name's Rhoda Mackay, and we've bought your old house."

A flicker of sharp interest showed in the old lady's eyes. "Oh?" she replied.

"Yes. It's a lovely house. And when we moved in, I found some pictures on the bedroom wall. They're of cats, and Danny says you love cats, so I thought you might like to have them back." She held out the package and smiled. "I love cats, too. I've got a Siamese called Opal, and she—"

Mrs Wilson interrupted her. "I don't want those old things," she said brusquely. "If I did, I wouldn't have left them behind." All the same, she had taken the pictures and was slowly thumbing through them. Coming to the black-and-white picture of the cat, she paused and her mouth twitched slightly, almost smiling. Rhoda grabbed the chance and said, "That's such a beautiful cat. Was it a tabby? And is that you in the background?"

The smile vanished. "Yes. Not that it's anything to you."

On the other side of the chair Danny raised his eyebrows in a "told you" sort of way.

Rhoda ignored him.

"Oh, but it is, Mrs Wilson," she persisted. "I love old pictures, you see, and—"

"You seem to love a lot of things," Mrs Wilson interrupted again. "Cats, old pictures, and being nosy." Suddenly she fixed Rhoda with a sharp, hostile glare. "What did you do with my armchair? I didn't want to leave that, but they wouldn't let me bring it. 'No room for it', they said. Absolute rubbish; of course there's room; they just don't want you to have anything that *they* don't control! Where is it, eh? I suppose your parents threw it away!"

"No, they didn't," Rhoda lied, not daring to look at Danny. "We really like it." She took a deep breath. "Did your son give it to you?"

There was a second's tense silence. Then Mrs Wilson said softly, "What?"

Rhoda swallowed. "Your son," she repeated. "I wondered if maybe he—"

"I haven't *got* a son!" Mrs Wilson's voice rose so violently and unexpectedly that Rhoda jumped back. "Do you hear me, girl – *do* you? *I haven't got a son!*"

Suddenly, shockingly, the old lady burst into tears. Across the room other residents stared in astonished curiosity, and Mrs Wilson thumped a clenched fist down on the chair.

"Go away, go away, you *horrible* children! Go away and leave me *alone!*"

The carer came hurrying in, followed by Matron, who had been passing, and while the carer tried to soothe Mrs Wilson, Matron hustled Rhoda and Danny out into the hall.

"What did you say to upset her?" she demanded angrily. "What have you done?"

Dismayed, Rhoda explained what had happened. She expected Matron just to shoo them out without another word – but to her surprise, Matron calmed down and frowned.

"That's very strange," she said thoughtfully. "As far as we know, Mrs Wilson hasn't got any family at all. But the other day she said something that puzzled us. She wasn't very well – a bit feverish – and one of the carers told me that she was mumbling about someone she called 'My David'. She said: 'It was all my fault and I never forgave him.' But when we tried to find out more, she went into her shell and wouldn't explain." She looked keenly at Rhoda. "We've known since she came here that poor Mrs Wilson's very unhappy about *something*, but she won't tell us what it is. If you can find any-thing else – maybe something at the house – that might give us a clue, I'd very much like to know about it." She paused. "Do you think you can try?"

Rhoda thought of Sheba. Slowly, she nodded.

"Yes," she said. "I think perhaps we can."

11

"The chair's the key to it," said Rhoda. "I'm certain now. Somehow, we've got to find out what its secret is."

"There's not much of it left to find out about," Danny pointed out. They were in Rhoda's garden, among the shrubs where the armchair was hidden, and he poked at the blackened frame with a piece of twig he'd broken off a buddleia bush.

"I know. But Sheba keeps leading me back to it." Rhoda's brow creased and she chewed her lower lip. "I can't help thinking. . ." She didn't finish, and Danny prompted,

"Thinking what?"

"I don't know. It sounds daft, but . . . I keep thinking it ought to be back in its old place, in the house."

"Oh, great! And what would your mum say about *that*?"

She sighed. "That's the problem. She'd throw a wobbler; I mean, she doesn't even know it's still here. But I'm *sure* that's what we should do."

A rustle in the undergrowth announced Opal. She emerged from the bushes, shook her head, and rubbed herself against Rhoda's legs.

"I know, Opie, it's so difficult, isn't it?" Rhoda said to her. "What do *you* think?"

Danny was just starting to say, "Don't be so dumb; she can't understand!" when Opal answered. She gave a long-drawn cry that rose up and down the scale, then she turned and, in a single leap, sprang on to the chair. Balancing on one of the arms she lifted her head and yowled again – then she took another flying leap to the ground, and dived back into the bushes. Peering through, they saw her streaking away in the direction of the house.

And beside her, as she ran, a small, ghostly shape kept pace before vanishing like smoke as Opal ran in at the back door.

Danny blinked rapidly. "I didn't see that. . . I *can't* have done!"

"You did," said Rhoda softly. "And so did I."

"But in broad daylight. . ."

"Why not? Why should ghosts only be able to appear at night? Sheba's trying to show us, Danny. She and Opal." The two cats weren't enemies any more, Rhoda thought. Since the armchair was burned, Opal seemed to have taken Sheba's side, as if she understood what Sheba wanted – what she *needed* – and was trying to help.

But Rhoda and Danny still had to play their parts. Opal and Sheba had shown them what was wanted. The trouble was, how could it be done?

Rhoda turned to Danny. "Look," she said, "I don't know how we're going to manage this, but we've *got* to find a way. I'm going to think very hard about it, and I want you to think, too. Between us we should be able to come up with something."

Danny scuffed the ground with one foot. "I'll

try," he said. "But I don't think we've got much chance. In fact I reckon it's pretty hopeless." He looked up. "Besides, there's something you haven't thought about."

"What?"

He grimaced. "Today's Tuesday. Guess what happens on Thursday?"

"Thursday. . . ?" Then it clicked. "Oh, no! School!"

Rhoda had completely forgotten about the new term. Amid all the excitement that was going on it had seemed light-years away; but it had crept up on them and now it loomed like a dark cloud.

"There won't be any time for thinking," said Danny. "What with you having to settle in, and homework and all the rest of it."

Rhoda stared at the armchair, but without really seeing it. "There'll have to be time," she said. "I don't care what else happens. There'll *have* to."

Sheba was quiet for the rest of that day and all through Wednesday. It was as if she knew what Rhoda and Danny had achieved, and she was no longer impatient but was peacefully

119

waiting for the next move.

But on Thursday, everything changed.

Rhoda's first day at her new school didn't go too well. It wasn't that there was anything wrong with the school itself – apart from the plain, boring fact that it *was* school – but right now she was resenting every moment she had to spend away from the house and the riddle of the armchair. That got her into trouble from the start, because she couldn't concentrate on anything as mundane as maths or English, and her lack of attention made her classmates think she was stand-offish. Danny had his own friends, and even on the school bus there was no chance to talk to him; so by the time she got home, Rhoda was thoroughly fed up.

Then the trouble began.

Sheba, it seemed, didn't realize why Rhoda could no longer give all her time and energy to what *she* wanted. Or if she did realize, she wasn't prepared to put up with it. The attacks started almost as soon as Rhoda came in. She was in the kitchen getting herself a cold drink when she heard a hiss and an instant later invisible needles clawed at her leg.

"*Oww!*" Rhoda jumped, then stared down at

the empty floor. "Sheba! Stop it!"

A soft growl was her only answer, and a small shadow seemed to flicker in the corner by the cooker. Five minutes later Sheba did it again, drawing blood this time. And from then on she kept up a barrage of small but painful assaults. In the kitchen and the sitting-room, on the stairs – especially on the stairs, because the attacks were more frightening in the gloom of the stairwell and landing. It got to the point where Rhoda was as jumpy as a cat herself.

At last it seemed that her only hope of getting away from Sheba was to have a shower. Cats disliked getting wet, so the bathroom was the one place where the angry ghost surely wouldn't follow her. Rhoda shut the bathroom door and stood looking and listening hard for a few seconds. Nothing. No tell-tale shadows, no soft, menacing noises . . . she'd escaped, and could have a few minutes' peace and quiet.

She got into the shower and stood shampooing her hair under the stream of warm water. Her nerves were jangling and her legs were sore where Sheba had scratched them. Better put some antiseptic on the

121

scratches, she thought. At least Mum hadn't noticed. If she did, she'd think it was Opal, and then. . .

The thought slid away into a lurching jolt of her heart as a shadow loomed suddenly on the shower curtain.

"Mum. . .?" Rhoda ventured nervously. But it couldn't be Mum. She'd locked the bathroom door; no one else could get in. And anyway, the shadow was much too small to be human. . .

Rhoda held her breath, listening, but the combination of the running water and shampoo in her ears made it impossible for her to hear anything outside the cubicle. She could see the shadow moving beyond the curtain. Prowling. It was *very* small. Cat-sized, in fact. . .

Sheba had come looking for her.

"Go away, will you?" Rhoda hissed through clenched teeth. "Leave me alone! I'm trying my best, but I can't help having to go to school!"

The shadow writhed and she thought she heard an answering growl, but it was impossible to be sure. Why wouldn't Sheba understand? It wasn't Rhoda's fault that she couldn't devote every moment of every day to solving the mystery! Now she'd have to run the gauntlet of the ghost-cat's fury again. Sheba would be lying in wait when she came out of the shower. Waiting to pounce. And the towel and all her clothes were out there, so she wouldn't have anything to protect her from another attack. It wasn't *fair*.

Feeling very edgy now, she finished washing her hair, sponged herself all over, then turned off the water. It gurgled away down the drainhole and she took a deep breath, bracing herself for what was inevitably about to happen. The bathroom seemed very quiet now. Sheba wasn't making a sound; but Rhoda knew she was there.

"All right," she said aloud. "I'm coming out. *Please*, Sheba, don't go for me again – I've had enough!"

She reached out to grasp the shower curtain and pull it back.

There was a slight sound behind her –

And with a ferocious yowl, an unseen weight hurled itself at the back of Rhoda's neck, driving its claws savagely into her shoulders.

Rhoda's scream brought Mum *and* Dad running. Dad hammered on the bathroom door, yelling, "Rho! Rho, are you all right?" and Mum was shouting her name too. When Rhoda managed to open the door at last, they both burst in to find her wrapped in her towel and dripping water all over the floor. Her face was dead-white and she was shaking.

"Rho!" Mum cried. "What happened?"

With a huge effort Rhoda pulled herself together. "It's – it's OK," she stammered. "I just – turned the shower on too hot. Didn't mean to scare you. Sorry."

It was a piece of quick thinking. Mum fussed, of course, convinced she must have scalded herself, and insisted on having a good look at her. She saw the scratches on Rhoda's shoulders, and Rhoda had to pretend that Opal had got stuck in the apple tree earlier and had clawed her while being rescued. She wasn't sure whether Mum believed that; but finally, with a few last, suspicious glances over her shoulder, Mum seemed to accept the explanation and went away. Rhoda stood in the middle of the bathroom floor. She knew Sheba was still there. She could *feel* her presence. Lurking. Waiting.

"All right, you little rat-bag," Rhoda whispered furiously to the invisible cat. "I know you can hear me, so you'd better listen! If you ever do that again – *ever* – then you can forget any idea of me helping you! That will be *it*!"

Silence. Had Sheba understood? Rhoda would have bet a week's allowance that she had. But whether it would make any difference. . .

She jumped at the slightest sound or movement as she rubbed herself dry, expecting Sheba to attack again at any moment. But perhaps the cat *had* taken notice. Sheba stayed around, and when she went into her bedroom to find clean clothes Rhoda could sense her following. But she didn't do anything else. She'd made her point, it seemed, and that was enough.

For now.

Though what would happen if she had to wait much longer for what she wanted, was something Rhoda didn't want to think about.

Sheba was running out of patience.

And Rhoda and Danny were running out of time.

12

After the ruckus in the shower, Sheba changed tactics.

She didn't attack Rhoda again. Instead, she took to following her, relentlessly and deliberately, wherever she went in or around the house. Rhoda never saw her and almost never heard her, except for an occasional faint hiss or growl. But she was constantly *aware* of her. It was as if the tabby cat was able to project the sense of her presence into Rhoda's mind – and she kept up the pressure. Even at night Rhoda could feel her in her room, staring invisibly from the desk or the window ledge or even the end of the bed. She didn't *do* anything any more. But in a way this new game of wits and nerves was even worse. At least Rhoda had had some breathing spaces between clawing attacks; now, though, the only time she was free of Sheba was when she was at school. And she still had the unpleasant feeling that, sooner or later, Sheba's patience would run out and she'd do something really drastic.

By the middle of the following week, Rhoda was just about ready to snap. She'd hardly spoken to Danny, except at the weekend; and even then he hadn't been much use. Oh yes, he'd been thinking about their problem. But he hadn't come up with any solutions. Rhoda couldn't really grumble about that; she hadn't done any better herself. But, as she pointed out, Danny didn't have Sheba breathing down his neck, so to speak, from morning to night. Much more of this, she added, and one of these days she'd just run away to Australia or something, and leave them both to it.

As it turned out, it was travel that finally broke the deadlock. Nothing as extreme as Australia, but over breakfast on Wednesday morning, Dad announced that he had to drive up to Glasgow on business. He'd be away from next Monday through to Thursday, he said, and Mum was going with him. It was a great chance for her to see her parents and her sisters, who all lived near the city.

Rhoda's eyes lit up. "Brilliant!" she said enthusiastically. "I haven't seen Gran and Grandad for ages either, and—"

"Hang on, Rho," Dad interrupted. "Sorry, love, but I'm afraid you'll have to stay behind."

Her face fell. "Dad! What do you mean?"

"You can't miss nearly a week of school when term's only just started," Dad told her, in one of those voices that said he'd made his mind up and wasn't going to budge. "Especially as it's a new school and I expect you've got some catching up to do."

"But—"

"No, Rho, there's no point arguing about it," Mum put in. "We've already talked to Mrs Downing next door, and she says you can stay with them; they've got a spare room while Danny's brothers are at college." She paused. "I thought you'd be *pleased*. You usually can't wait to get away from us; and last time we took you to see your grandparents you were bored stiff. Anyway, you and Danny get on all right, don't you?"

Rhoda couldn't tell them that the only reason she really wanted to go to Scotland was to get away from Sheba. She could feel the ghost cat sitting beside her chair at this very moment, staring resolutely at her. Even dreary relatives had to be better than that.

But then another thought slipped into her mind.

"Well . . . I can still come into the house, can't I?" she said. "I mean, I don't suppose Mrs Downing'll want Opal around, and she'll have to be fed, and let in and out."

"Of course you can come in," said Mum. "You're old enough to be sensible, so you'll only have to eat and sleep next door."

"But no parties," Dad added warningly. "And that includes 'just a few mates', right? We're not having any of that, and we've said so to the Downings, so they'll be checking."

"Fat chance," said Rhoda. "I haven't *got* any mates round here yet."

"Well, there's another reason not to miss school," Mum pointed out. "Right; that's settled, then."

So it was. And the thought that had hit Rhoda took shape – because this was the chance she and Danny had been waiting for.

Rhoda didn't know how she got through the next few days. She had to pretend not to be excited; if Mum or Dad became suspicious, they'd assume she *was* planning to have a riotous party, and they'd probably cancel their whole trip. What Rhoda actually had in mind would have scared them even more if they'd come anywhere near guessing it. But they wouldn't guess. Not in a million years.

She and Danny started to make plans. They both felt instinctively that what they had to do would be better done after dark; which, as Danny pointed out, might cause problems with his parents. But there was a disco in the village hall on Tuesday night. They could pretend they were going, and provided they didn't switch on any lights in Rhoda's house they should be safe. Then, all they would have to do was install Mrs Wilson's armchair back in its old place; and with luck, Sheba would do the rest.

Sheba was as keyed-up as Rhoda as the day for Mum and Dad's departure drew nearer. Several times Rhoda heard her purring, and once she thought Mum heard it too, for she started suddenly and paused, listening and frowning. But Sheba had the sense not to let that happen a second time.

Opal, too, was edgy and excitable. She kept agitating to go out, then making hurtling rushes down the garden, past the apple tree and into the bushes where she crashed around for some minutes before reappearing, eyes wild and tail lashing, and tearing back into the house like a whirlwind. Every evening she plonked herself squarely in front of the sitting-room hearth, in the exact spot where the arm-chair had stood, and refused to move until Rhoda went to bed, when she followed her up to her room and settled on the ledge. Opal knew exactly what was going on, and she was as impatient as Sheba.

Monday came at last. Rhoda didn't know how she managed to appear normal as she said goodbye to Mum and Dad and went to catch the school bus. They were leaving at about ten; by the time she got home they'd probably have arrived at the other end. They had promised to phone – which meant she could be sure they really were in Glasgow and hadn't turned back for some reason – and she and Danny would be in the clear. Tonight, they'd move the armchair back into the house. Then tomorrow. . .

Luckily for them both, Mrs Downing was a bit vague, not the sort of person to ask too many awkward questions. So that evening it was easy to find an excuse for "messing about" in Rhoda's garden.

Dusk was falling as they manoeuvred the chair out of its hiding place and carried it to the house. Shadows had gathered and lengthened, and Rhoda half expected to catch a glimpse of Sheba gliding behind them. The ghost cat didn't appear. But Opal was waiting in the sitting-room, and when she saw the chair coming in she got to her feet and came running to them, rubbing ecstatically round their ankles as if to say, "Yes, yes, this is what we want!"

They put the chair down and stood looking at it for a minute. Then Danny said,

"Right. Now all we've got to do is wait."

The chair looked strange and out of place, Rhoda thought. It wasn't just that it had been ruined by the fire; it seemed, already, to belong to the past; to someone else's life. This is nothing to do with us, she thought with a small shiver. Are we really doing the right thing?

A chilly little breath blew through the room, and something soft, that wasn't Opal, seemed to brush against her leg.

"All right." She spoke aloud, but not to Danny. "Tomorrow, then. Roll on to-morrow. . ."

Tuesday was one of those changeable, unpredictable spring days. Rhoda got on the school bus in bright sunshine, got off it in pouring rain, and spent the morning and lunch breaks dodging showers that, she was convinced, had just been lurking in wait.

After lunch there was a sudden brief but spectacular thunderstorm, then the sun came out again and by the time school ended it was almost hot. Danny had a late class, so Rhoda went home alone. Opal greeted her with a lot of indignant complaints about the weather, ate a large dish of food and then scooted up the apple tree and came back soaking wet a few minutes later. The Siamese was skittish and excitable, and Rhoda felt much the same as she checked the sitting-room for the last time, to make sure everything was ready. She and Danny had pushed the rest of the furniture back against the walls and the chair stood waiting in solitary splendour. For once, Rhoda couldn't sense Sheba.

Tea at the Downings seemed to drag on for hours, but at last it was late enough to go home and "get ready for the disco". To keep up the pretence Rhoda did actually change into her new jeans and a glittery Lycra top; and half an hour later Danny came round.

"OK." He too had dressed up to avert his parents' suspicions. "We'll go out of the front gate in case anyone's looking, then nip round the back and climb over the fence. Got a torch ready?"

"In the kitchen." Rhoda was going round closing the curtains, which were thick enough to ensure that torchlight in the house wouldn't be visible from outside. Pausing, she peered through one of the windows. "Sky's getting murky again. We might get another storm."

"Great." Danny grinned. "Dark, creepy house with lightning flickering. Classic horror-movie stuff!"

"Don't!" she said. "I'm jumpy enough already."

They turned all the lights off and made a show of leaving, banging the front gate and talking loudly as they headed off down the lane. A rough path led off the lane and curved round to the rear of the houses; turning on to it, they doubled back and scrambled over the garden fence where the bushes were at their thickest.

"Mum's shut our curtains," Danny said, looking. "Good. Come on – and keep low."

Crouching, and feeling faintly silly, they made a dash for Rhoda's house.

"Don't let the door slam!" Rhoda warned as Danny slipped into the kitchen at her heels. "Shut it quietly, that's it – ow! Oh, it's you, Opie!"

Opal had heard them and come running to investigate; she was nearly invisible in the gloom and Rhoda had stumbled over her. The Siamese made a loud, questioning sort of noise, and Rhoda hastened to soothe her.

"Shh! Quiet, Opie, don't make so much noise! It's only us." Kicking off her shoes, which had noisy heels, she padded to the sitting-room. Danny picked up the torch and followed.

At the door Rhoda paused. The room looked different somehow; changed even from a mere few minutes ago. With every curtain in the house drawn there was hardly any light at all, and the shifted furniture formed strange, looming shapes, unfamiliar and a little disturbing. But there was more to it than that. Something about the atmosphere . . . there was a feeling of suspense, tension. Something *waiting*.

A peculiar little shiver ran down Rhoda's spine. Hoping that Danny hadn't noticed it, she took a deep breath and made herself walk forward, into the room. It was cold. *Very* cold. And there was the armchair, alone by the hearth.

"Which one of us is going to do it?" she whispered.

Danny didn't answer for a few moments. Then: "You." She looked over her shoulder at him and he added, "It's your house, after all."

The reasoning wasn't convincing, but Danny was as scared as she was. Rhoda nodded.

"All right, then." She moved forward again.

Everything was suddenly very, very quiet. In fact she could only hear one faint sound, and at first she didn't know what it was. But then she recognized it. Rain, pattering on the garden outside and blowing against the windows. It almost sounded like a cat purring.

From far in the distance came a low, threatening rumble of thunder. Danny had been right, then. Rhoda hoped the storm was moving away rather than towards them. She wasn't afraid of it but, as she had said, the horror-movie scenario would be a bit *too* much.

Danny switched on the torch and shone it in the direction of the armchair. It was meant to reassure Rhoda, but it had the opposite effect, for it reminded her of her dream; the shaft of moonlight slanting in at the window and illuminating the chair like a stage spotlight. Rhoda gulped, not liking the memory. But she couldn't bring herself to tell him. Heart bumping, she stepped up to the armchair. For a second or two she looked at it. Then, slowly and carefully, she turned and sat down on the ruined seat. . .

13

"She's here," Rhoda said softly.

Danny looked cautiously around, then replied as quietly, "I can't see anything. . ."

"I know. But I can feel her." She shifted in the chair, trying to pretend it wasn't uncomfortable, and whispered:

"Sheba? Come on, Sheba. We're here. We're ready."

There was no response, but she knew the tabby cat was somewhere close by. "Danny, turn the torch off," she said. "I don't think Sheba likes it."

Danny flicked the switch. The room sank

into gloom – and, like a patch of dark mist in the corner, Sheba appeared and padded silently towards the chair. Her eyes glowed strangely; they weren't amber now, like a living cat's eyes, but looked silver-grey, almost colourless. Reaching Rhoda's feet she stopped and looked up. They saw her mouth open, but when she meowed there was no sound.

"Come on, Sheba." Rhoda patted her own knees. "Come on."

Sheba's tail twitched. She meowed silently again, then started to pace round the chair. Round and round, once, twice – but now her tail was lashing fiercely, and the fur along her spine bristled.

"What's the matter with her?" Danny breathed.

"She's angry about something." But what? Rhoda was baffled – had they upset Sheba in some way? Had they done something wrong? If only they could *understand*!

Suddenly Sheba spun round. Her ears went back, then her front paws flashed out and she attacked one of the armchair's legs. Rhoda distinctly heard the sound of her claws raking the blackened wood and she hissed, "Sheba, what *is* it? What's wrong?"

The ghost cat fixed her with an extra-ordinary, baleful stare. Then her tail lashed one final time – and she vanished.

"*Sheba!*" Rhoda cried.

"Shh!" Danny warned. "Mum and Dad'll hear you!"

Rhoda swallowed back a second cry and they both looked wildly around the room for Sheba. But Sheba had gone without trace.

"I don't understand," Danny said, almost angrily. "We try to do exactly what she wants, and she reacts like this!"

Rhoda touched his arm. "Danny – look at Opal."

Opal had been crouching in the kitchen doorway since they came in, watching them but not making any move. Now, though, she was on her feet, staring fixedly at the floor beneath the chair.

"Opie?" Rhoda ventured.

A small, rumbling growl came from Opal's throat.

"That's what she kept doing when we first came here," Rhoda said.

"She's looking at the same spot where

Sheba scratched the chair leg," Danny pointed out.

Opal stood up. She walked to the hearth and began to prowl up and down. Her tail was bristling, and suddenly Rhoda began to feel very nervous. She tried to get a grip on the feeling and squash it down, but it was growing and she couldn't control it. Something was building up, she knew it, she *knew* it –

Then, without any warning, a vivid flash seared through the room.

"*Ahh!*" Rhoda almost leaped out of the arm-chair, and her yelp of shock was drowned by a roar of thunder.

"*Ohh. . .*" she started to gasp – then stopped, staring at Danny. "What? What is it?"

Danny was staring, too. Straight at her. "In the lightning," he said. "I saw something."

"*What*, for God's sake?" The rain had increased in force, hammering on the ground now, and the windows rattled as a gust of wind shook them.

"I – don't know. It was on your lap. But it wasn't Sheba."

Rhoda leaped out of the chair as if she'd

been scalded. "*What did you see?*" Her voice rose to a squeak.

Danny was staring at the chair. He licked his lips. "Have you got any candles?"

"In the cupboard, over there." Rhoda pointed. She was still shaking.

"OK," said Danny. "Then I think we should light some."

Three more lightning flashes shivered through the room while they were finding the candles. Rhoda fetched some matches from the kitchen; when she came back, Danny had set the candles on the floor, in a circle around the armchair. As he lit them one by one, the room lifted from murky darkness into quavering light and shadow.

And Rhoda saw what he had seen.

On the blackened seat of the armchair was what appeared to be a bundle of papers.

"*What?*" The sight was so bizarre that Rhoda could hardly believe it. "Where did *they* come from?"

Danny stepped forward, stretching out one hand. His fingers touched the papers . . . and went straight through them. "They're a mirage," he said softly. "There's nothing really there at all."

"What does it *mean*?"

Before Danny could even try to answer that, there was a small, flickering disturbance near the fireplace, and Sheba reappeared. She padded to the chair and stood looking up for a moment. Then she jumped on to the seat, raised her head and opened her mouth, as though uttering a long, loud wail, though no sound was audible.

As though it were a signal, the other ghostly cats appeared. They gathered round the two humans, staring at them as though trying silently to tell them something. Lightning flashed again, turning the room electric blue and momentarily blinding Rhoda and Danny. When their vision cleared, the image of the papers on the armchair had vanished. But the cats were still there – and they were moving, closing in until Rhoda could feel the cold, phantom touch of their fur. With a shock she realized that the cats were slowly but relentlessly pushing her and Danny, forcing them to move across the floor.

"What the—" Danny's face had turned white.

"Don't fight them!" Rhoda whispered. "Do what they want!"

The cats continued to push, and now Opal had joined them, adding her own real weight to their efforts. She was meowing, over and over again, and as Rhoda and Danny shuffled another step and then another, her cries became more urgent.

Until, suddenly, the pushing stopped.

Rhoda looked towards the armchair. Sheba was still there on the seat, but now she was purring, the noise of it audible even above another grumble of thunder. Then she jumped down, ran to Rhoda, and clawed the floor by her feet.

"Danny," Rhoda whispered, "give me the torch. . ."

He handed it over and she dropped to her knees, the cats gathering round her like chilly little breaths of wind. The torchlight's bright circle glared on the floorboards, and Rhoda began to run her hands over them, searching, looking. The boards were scuffed and stained and full of knotholes.

But there was something that *wasn't* a knothole. It had been made deliberately. And this floorboard was shorter than the others, and loose . . .

It came up with astonishing ease. Rhoda lifted it aside – and she and Danny gazed in amazement at what was revealed beneath.

In the open space under the floor was a bundle of papers, tied with a piece of ribbon. Carefully Rhoda drew them out. Some were old, brittle and yellowed at the edges; others were newer.

A shiver went through Rhoda. With unsteady hands she untied the ribbon and spread the papers out on the floor. Every one was in an envelope, with stamp and postmark, and they were all addressed to "Mrs Grace Wilson". There were Christmas cards, birthday cards, letters, postcards. Rhoda turned a postcard over. It began: "Dear Mum".

The sound of the cats' purring rose to a crescendo. They were all pressing around her now, Opal in their midst. Then came another flicker of lightning, another peal of thunder –

And there was only Opal, purring and purring and purring.

14

For more than an hour, as the storm slowly faded away in the distance, Rhoda and Danny pored by candle-light over the sheaf of papers from under the floorboards. And slowly, like a jigsaw puzzle, they pieced together Mrs Wilson's poignant story.

Mrs Wilson *did* have a family. The earliest greetings cards they found dated right back to the 1960s, and were all signed "From your loving son David". Then, years later, they became "From David and Meg"; and the newest ones of all were from "David, Meg and the children".

But it was the letters that revealed the real truth. Every one was from David, and in them he pleaded with his mother to relent. Rhoda and Danny understood, now, why Mrs Wilson had quarrelled with her son. He was her only child, and when her husband died he was all she had left. She became possessive and jealous, and when David met Meg, she had seen her as a rival who wanted to steal him away. She had tried to break up the relationship, and when that failed she forced David to choose between her and his girlfriend. David had chosen Meg – and Mrs Wilson had never forgiven him. Through all the years that followed, David had tried to persuade his mother to change. Every birthday, every Christmas, he sent her loving cards; and time and again he wrote to her begging her to unbend. But Mrs Wilson refused. Stubbornly, she had ignored his letters – though she kept every one of them – and she had never met her daughter-in-law, or seen her grandchildren.

Rhoda was in tears by the time they finished. She hid it from Danny, feeling a complete idiot; but the story touched her to the heart. Poor, foolish Mrs Wilson – so lonely for so many years, and all because of her own pride. And now, it was too late to change anything.

Danny had finished looking through the papers and was sitting back on his heels, frowning. Then suddenly he picked up the torch and shone it into the hole in the floor.

"There's something else in there," he said.

"What?" Rhoda looked as, reaching in, Danny drew out another envelope.

"It wasn't tied up with the others," he said. "And it's different, look. It isn't *from* David; it's *to* him."

The envelope was sealed and stamped but, unlike the others, the stamp bore no postmark and the envelope had not been opened.

"It was never posted," Rhoda said softly. "Do you think. . . ?"

The sentence trailed off. Danny was tearing at the envelope, and Rhoda's instinctive thought that they were prying into something too private slid away.

There was a letter inside, several pages long, and handwritten. It was dated a few months ago; just before Mrs Wilson had gone into the home.

It began: "My dearest David. . ."

Rhoda and Danny read the letter together, in total silence, as the final piece of the jigsaw slipped into place. Mrs Wilson *had* relented at last. She had written to her son, wanting to make peace and asking him to forgive her for her harshness and unkindness. She loved him, she said, and had missed him dreadfully for all these years. Now, she longed to see him again, and meet his wife and his children. But she was so ashamed, and afraid that even if David would forgive her, Meg might not.

The last paragraph brought a lump to Rhoda's throat. It said:

"I am very sad at the moment because I have just lost my dear cat. She was called Sheba, and she was the last descendant of the little kitten you gave me nearly forty years ago. I cannot have another one, because I would not be able to look after it now that I am leaving. I loved Sheba very much, as I loved all my cats, because they made me feel close to you. If only they could talk, I know they would have told me what a fool I have been."

"Oh, dear. . ." Rhoda sniffed and wiped her eyes. "That's so *sad*."

Danny blinked. He, too, was more affected

than he wanted to admit.

"Look," he said, "maybe there's something we can do. . ."

She glanced at him keenly. "What do you mean?"

"Well, it's what Sheba and the other cats want, isn't it? Like she says; if they could talk, they'd have told her. Mrs Wilson wanted to send this letter, only she was too scared. But the cats knew it was here. They *wanted* her to send it, so they used us as – as kind of go-betweens." He breathed a gusty sigh. "It's crazy, isn't it? So weird, no one would believe us if we told them."

"Even Mrs Wilson?" said Rhoda.

"Well . . . maybe. Or maybe not."

Rhoda looked at the letter again. "We've got David's address," she said slowly, thoughtfully. "It'd be easy to get the phone number. . ."

The candles flickered then, briefly. A peculiar little breeze seemed to flit through the room. And Opal started to purr. Rhoda and Danny exchanged a glance. Then Danny smiled.

"It's your house," he said. "And your phone. . ."

15

On Wednesday evening, Rhoda and Danny had been watching from the window for an hour when the car at last drew up at the gate. Turning to each other with broad grins, they slapped their hands together in silent high-fives, then ran for the front door.

They met David and Meg Wilson half-way up the path. For a moment Rhoda couldn't believe that this man, older than her dad and with greying hair, was the same person she had seen in the garden vision, and it nearly brought on a fit of the giggles. Meg, she thought, looked a bit like Mum. And they were both smiling broadly.

"You must be Rhoda and Danny," David Wilson greeted them. "Hello!" He shook hands, then his face sobered as he added, "We've both got a lot to thank you for."

Over a cup of tea (Rhoda made awful tea but the Wilsons didn't seem to mind) and a cake bought on the way home from school, they heard all that had happened since Rhoda had nervously made her phone call last night. David had been astonished to hear the story she had to tell. He had eagerly asked her to read the letter to him, and when she did so he was thrilled. He and Meg only lived fifty miles away, he said; they would drive down as soon as possible, go straight to the home and see his mother. And so they had done. They didn't say too much about the reunion; that, after all, was something very private. But the little they did say was enough to tell Rhoda that Sheba's wish had come true.

"It's incredible that you found the letters after all this time," David said.

"Well. . ." Rhoda didn't dare look at Danny. "It was just luck, I suppose. Mum's going to have carpets fitted, so I was kind of getting the floor ready, and one of the boards was loose, and. . ." The words fizzled out as she realized that she must sound like some kind of prim little goody-goody, and Danny gave a snort of laughter that he tried, not very successfully, to disguise as a cough.

David smiled. "However it happened, it was a piece of wonderful luck for us. And for Mum." The smile widened. "The children are coming to see her next week. Not that they *are* children now; they're both grown up. She's looking forward to that so much, and so are they. And it's all thanks to you two."

Rhoda returned the smile, then at last glanced at Danny. He was looking back at her, and she knew they were both thinking the same thing: *It isn't really anything to do with us at all. But that's a secret we'll never tell.*

The Wilsons left a few minutes later. Rhoda and Danny waved them off, then went back into the house and shut the door.

"*Phoo. . .*" Rhoda let her breath out and leaned against the front door. Danny grinned and said, "How does it feel to be sleuth, a social worker and a Fairy Godmother all rolled into one?"

"Oh, shut up!" But she grinned back.

"We'd better go round to my place," Danny said. "Tea'll be ready. Not that I can eat much, after all that cake."

"Me neither. But before we go, there's one more thing we've got to do."

"Ah. . ." said Danny. "Yeah, there is." He paused. "How do you think Sheba's going to take it?"

"I don't know. I honestly don't." Rhoda's face was serious now. Then the ghost of a smile appeared. "There's only one way to find out, isn't there?"

They'd put the old armchair just outside the back door, as it would have been hard to explain its charred state to the Wilsons. Now, it had to go back to the end of the garden, where Dad would probably chop it up for firewood. Sheba's chair. Would she be angry? Or was the chair's purpose – and Sheba's – now over and done. . .?

They trooped through to the garden and stood looking at the chair.

"Poor old thing," Rhoda said. She patted the blackened wood. "But I don't think Sheba needs you any more."

As they carried the chair down the garden, they looked for signs of Sheba. But no ghostly little shape appeared, and no mysterious sounds disturbed the quiet dusk. Rhoda wondered where Opal was. She had come in to the sitting-room when the Wilsons first arrived, looked at them for a few seconds and then gone silently away, and they hadn't seen her since.

Past the remains of the bonfire and into the bushes they carried the old chair. They put it down, and Rhoda turned, gazing around. Nothing moved. The shadows were empty. And suddenly she knew with a sure instinct that this really was the end of the story.

Danny was already pushing his way back through the bushes, but Rhoda lingered. "Goodbye, Sheba," she whispered softly. "I'll miss you."

She didn't see anything. But just for a moment she felt a small, soft, furry touch against her leg, as if a cat was rubbing affectionately. And she seemed to hear purring. Quiet, contented purring, that echoed faintly in her ears and faded away into silence.

"Come on, Rhoda!" Danny yelled from the

other side of the bushes.

Rhoda's magical moment dissolved and vanished. She smiled. She grinned. Then she plunged through the tangled branches, emerging on to the lawn. As she did so, a loud, imperious squawk came from the apple tree, and Rhoda looked up to see Opal clawing her way down the trunk. She looked smugger than ever, and another squawk proudly announced, "Look at me, aren't I brilliant!"

"Come here, you crazy animal!" Rhoda reached up and Opal scrambled on to her shoulder, where she balanced like an acrobat and purred noisily in her ear.

"Come *on*!" Danny was half-way up the garden, fists on hips, waiting for her. "Talking to cats – you're as bad as old Mrs Wilson!"

Rhoda stuck her tongue out at him, trying to ignore the fact that Opal was now blithely kneading her neck with *very* sharp claws.

"Not quite!" she said.